PENGUIN BOOKS
UNTOUCHABLE

Mulk Raj Anand, one of the most highly regarded Indian novelists writing in English, was born in Peshawar in 1905. He was educated at the universities of Lahore, London and Cambridge, and lived in England for many years, finally settling in a village in Western India after the war. His main concern has always been for 'the creatures in the lower depths of Indian society who once were men and women: the rejected, who had no way to articulate their anguish against the oppressors'. His novels on humanism have been translated into several world languages.

The fiction-factions include *Untouchable* (1935), *Coolie* (1936), *Two Leaves and a Bud* (1937), *The Village* (1939), *Across the Black Waters* (1940), *The Sword and the Sickle* (1942)—and the much acclaimed *Private Life of an Indian Prince* (1953). His autobiographical novels, *Seven Summers* (1950), *Morning Face* (1968), which won the National Academy Award, *Confession of a Lover* (1972) and *The Bubble* (1988), reveal the story of his experiments with truth and the struggle of his various egos to attain a possible higher self.

'One of the most eloquent and imaginative works to deal with this difficult and emotive subject.'
—Martin Seymour-Smith on *Untouchable*

D1490503

MULK RAJ ANAND

UNTOUCHABLE

PENGUIN BOOKS

PENGUIN BOOKS

Published by the Penguin Group

Penguin Books India Pvt. Ltd, 11 Community Centre, Panchsheel Park, New Delhi 110 017, India

Penguin Group (USA) Inc., 375 Hudson Street, New York, New York 10014, USA

Penguin Group (Canada), 90 Eglinton Avenue East, Suite 700, Toronto, Ontario, M4P 2Y3, Canada (a division of Pearson Penguin Canada Inc.)

Penguin Books Ltd, 80 Strand, London WC2R 0RL, England

Penguin Ireland, 25 St Stephen's Green, Dublin 2, Ireland (a division of Penguin Books Ltd)

Penguin Group (Australia), 250 Camberwell Road, Camberwell, Victoria 3124, Australia (a division of Pearson Australia Group Pty Ltd)

Penguin Group (NZ), 67 Apollo Drive, Rosedale, North Shore 0632, New Zealand (a division of Pearson New Zealand Ltd)

Penguin Group (South Africa) (Pty) Ltd, 24 Sturdee Avenue, Rosebank, Johannesburg 2196, South Africa

Penguin Books Ltd, Registered Offices: 80 Strand, London WC2R 0RL, England

First published by Wishart 1935
First published by Penguin Books Ltd 1940
First published in India by Penguin Books India 2001

ISBN 9780143027805

The original edition of this novel was dedicated to Edith Young. In this edition I add the name of *Perspirer* K.S. Shelvankar and *Inspirer* Mahatma Gandhi.

This is a work of fiction. Names, characters, places and incidents are either the product of the author's imagination or are used fictitiously, and any resemblance to any actual person, living or dead, events or locales is entirely coincidental.

For sale in India, Bangladesh and Nepal only

Typeset in CG Times by SÜRYA, New Delhi
Printed at Pauls Press, New Delhi

PREFACE

Some years ago, I came across a copy of a book by myself, *A Passage to India*, which had apparently been read by an indignant Colonel. He had not concealed his emotions. On the front page, he had written, 'burn when done', and lower down: 'Has a dirty mind, see page 215'. I turned to page 215 with pardonable haste. There I found the words: 'The sweepers of Chandrapur had just struck, and half the commodes remained desolate in consequence.' This light-hearted remark has excluded me forever from military society ever since.

Well, if the Colonel thought *A Passage to India* dirty, what will he think about *Untouchable*, which describes a day in the life of a sweeper in an Indian city with every realistic circumstance. Is it a clean book or a dirty one? Some readers, especially those who consider themselves all-white, will go purple in the face with rage before they have finished a dozen pages, and will exclaim that they cannot trust themselves to speak. I cannot trust myself either, though for a different reason: the book seems to me indescribably clean and I hesitate for words in which this can be conveyed. Avoiding rhetoric and circumlocution, it has gone straight to the heart of its subject and purified it. None of us are pure—we shouldn't be alive if we were. But to the straightforward all things can become pure, and it is to the directness of his attack that Mr. Anand's success is probably due.

What a strange business has been made of this business of the human body relieving itself! The ancient Greeks did not worry about it, and they were the sanest and happiest of men. But both our civilisation and the Indian civilisation have got tied up in the most fantastic knots. Our own knot was only tied a hundred years ago, and some of us are hoping to undo it. It takes the form of prudishness and reticence; we have been trained from childhood to think excretion shameful, and grave evils have resulted both physical and psychological, with which modern education is just beginning to cope. The Indian tangle is of a different kind. Indians, like most Orientals, are refreshingly frank; they have none of our complexes about functioning, they accept the process as something necessary and natural, like sleep. On the other hand they have evolved a hideous nightmare unknown to the west: the belief that the products are ritually unclean as well as physically unpleasant, and that those who carry them away or otherwise help to dispose of them are outcastes from society. Really, it takes the human mind to evolve anything so devilish. No animal could have hit on it. As one of Mr. Anand's characters says: 'They think we are dirt because we clean their dirt.'

The sweeper is worse off than a slave, for the slave may change his master and his duties and may even become free, but the sweeper is bound for ever, born into a state from which he cannot escape and where he is excluded from social intercourse and the consolations of his religion. Unclean himself, he pollutes others when he touches them. They have to purify themselves, and to rearrange their plans for the day. Thus he is a disquieting as well as a disgusting object to the orthodox as he walks along the public roads, and it is his duty to call out and warn them that he is coming. No wonder that the dirt enters into his soul, and that he feels himself at moments to be what he is supposed to be. It is sometimes said that he is so degraded that he doesn't mind, but this is not the opinion of those who have studied his case, nor is it borne out by my own slight testimony: I remember on my visits to India noticing that the sweepers were more sensitive-looking and more personable than other servants, and I knew one who had some skill as a poet.

Untouchable could only have been written by an Indian, and by an Indian who observed from the outside. No European, however sympathetic, could have created the character of Bakha, because he would not have known enough about his troubles. And no Untouchable could have written the book, because he would have been involved in indignation and self-pity. Mr. Anand stands in the ideal position. By caste he is a Kshatriya, and he might have been expected to inherit the pollution-complex. But as a child he played with the children of the sweepers attached to an Indian regiment, he grew to be fond of them, and to understand a tragedy which he did not share. He has just the right mixture of insight and detachment, and the fact that he has come to fiction through philosophy has given him depth. It might have given him vagueness—that curse of the generalising mind—but his hero is no suffering abstraction. Bakha is a real individual, lovable, thwarted, sometimes grand, sometimes weak, and thoroughly Indian. Even his physique is distinctive; we can recognise his broad intelligent face, graceful torso and heavy buttocks, as he does his nasty jobs, or stumps out in artillery boots in hopes of a pleasant walk through the city with a paper of cheap sweets in his hand.

The book is simply planned, but it has form. The action occupies one day, and takes place in a small-area. The great catastrophe of the 'touching' (p. 46) occurs in the morning, and poisons all that happens subsequently, even such pleasant episodes as the hockey match and the country walk. After a jagged course of ups and downs, we come to the solution, or rather to the three solutions, with which the book closes. The first solution is that of Hutchinson, the Salvationist missionary: Jesus Christ. But though Bakha is touched at hearing that Christ receives all men, irrespective of caste, he gets bored, because the missionary cannot tell him who Christ is. Then follows the second solution, with the effect of a crescendo: Gandhi. Gandhi too says that all Indians are equal, and the account he gives of a Brahmin doing sweeper's work goes straight to the boy's heart. Hard upon this comes the third solution, put into the mouth of a modernist poet.

It is prosaic, straightforward, and considered in the light of what has gone before in the book, it is very convincing. No god is needed to rescue the Untouchables, no vows of self-sacrifice and abnegation on the part of more fortunate Indians, but simply and solely—the flush system. Introduce water-closets and main-drainage throughout India, and all this wicked rubbish about untouchability will disappear. Some readers may find this closing section of the book too voluble and sophisticated, in comparison with the clear observation which has preceded it, but it is an integral part of the author's scheme. It is the necessary climax, and it has mounted up with triple effect. Bakha returns to his father and his wretched bed, thinking now of the Mahatma, now of the Machine. His Indian day is over and the next day will be like it, but on the surface of the earth if not in the depths of the sky, a change is at hand.

E.M. Forster

UNTOUCHABLE

The outcastes' colony was a group of mud-walled houses that clustered together in two rows, under the shadow both of the town and the cantonment, but outside their boundaries and separate, from them. There lived the scavengers, the leather-workers, the washermen, the barbers, the water-carriers, the grass-cutters and other outcastes from Hindu society. A brook ran near the lane, once with crystal-clear water, now soiled by the dirt and filth of the public latrines situated about it, the odour of the hides and skins of dead carcases left to dry on its banks, the dung of donkeys, sheep, horses, cows and buffaloes heaped up to be made into fuel cakes, and the biting, choking, pungent fumes that oozed from its sides. The absence of a drainage system had, through the rains of various seasons, made of the quarter a marsh which gave out the most offensive stink. And altogether the ramparts of human and animal refuse that lay on the outskirts of this little colony, and the ugliness, the squalor and the misery which lay within it, made it an 'uncongenial' place to live in.

At least so thought Bakha, a young man of eighteen, strong and able-bodied, the son of Lakha, the Jemadar[1] of all the sweepers in the town and the cantonment, and officially in charge of the three rows of public latrines which lined the extremest end of the colony, by the brookside. But then he had been working in the barracks of a British regiment for some years on a sort of

---

[1]Head or Foreman.

probation with a remote uncle and had been caught by the glamour of the 'white man's' life. The Tommies had treated him as a human being and he had learnt to think of himself as superior to his fellow-outcastes. Otherwise, the rest of the outcastes, with the possible exception of Chota, the leather-worker's son, who oiled his hair profusely, and parted it like the Englishmen on one side, wore a pair of shorts at hockey and smoked cigarettes like them, and of Ram Charan, the washerman's son who aped Chota and Bakha in turn, were content with their lot.

Bakha thought of the uncongeniality of his home as he lay half awake in the morning of an autumn day, covered by a worn-out, greasy blanket, on a faded blue carpet which was spread on the floor in a corner of the twelve feet by five, dank, dingy, one-roomed mud-house. His sister slept on a cot next to him and his father and brother snored from under a patched, ochre-coloured quilt, on a broken string bed, further up.

The nights had been cold, as they always are in the town of Bulashah, as cold as the days are hot. And though, both during winter and summer, he slept with his day clothes on, the sharp, bitter wind that blew from the brook at dawn had penetrated to his skin, past the inadequate blanket, through the regulation overcoat, breeches, puttees and ammunition boots of the military uniform that clothed him.

He shivered as he turned on his side. But he didn't mind the cold very much, suffering it willingly because he could sacrifice a good many comforts for the sake of what he called 'fashun,' by which he understood the art of wearing trousers, breeches, coat, puttees, boots, etc., as worn by the British and Indian soldiers in India. 'You lover of your mother,' his father had once abusively said to him, 'take a quilt, spread a bedding on a string bed, and throw away that blanket of the *gora* white men; you will die of cold in that thin cloth.' But Bakha was a child of modern India. The clear-cut styles of European dress had impressed his naïve mind. This stark simplicity had furrowed his old Indian consciousness and cut deep new lines where all the considerations which made India evolve a skirty costume as best fitted for the human body, lay dormant. Bakha had looked at the Tommies, stared at them with wonder and amazement when he first went to live at the British regimental barracks with his uncle. He had had glimpses, during his sojourn there, of the life the Tommies lived, sleeping on strange, low canvas beds covered tightly with blankets, eating eggs, drinking tea and wine in tin mugs, going to parade and then walking down to the bazaar with cigarettes in their mouths and small silver-mounted canes in their hands. And he had soon become possessed with an overwhelming desire to live their life. He had been told they were sahibs, superior people. He had felt that to put on their clothes made one a sahib too. So he tried to copy them in everything, to copy them as well as he could in the exigencies of his peculiarly Indian circumstances. He had begged one Tommy for the gift of a pair of trousers. The man had given him a pair of breeches which he had to spare. A Hindu sepoy, for the good of his own soul, had been kind enough to make an endowment of a pair of boots and puttees. For the other items he had gone down to the rag-seller's shop in the town. He had looked longingly at that shop. Ever since he was a child he had walked past the wooden stall on which lay heaped the scarlet and khaki uniforms discarded or pawned by the Tommies, pith solar topees, peak caps, knives, forks, buttons, old books and other oddments of Anglo-Indian life. And he had hungered for the touch of them. But he had never mustered up courage enough to go up to the keeper of the shop and to ask him the price of anything, lest it should be a price he could not pay and lest the man should find out from his talk that he was a sweeper-boy. So he had stared and stared, stealthily noticing the variety of their queer, well-cut forms. 'I will look like a sahib,' he had secretly told himself. 'And I shall walk like them. Just as they do, in twos, with Chota as my companion. But I have no money to buy things.' And there his fantasy would break down and he would walk away from the shop rather crestfallen, with a heavy heart. Then he had had the good luck to come by some money at the British barracks. The pay which he received there had, of course, to be given to his father, but the bakshish which he had collected from the Tommies amounted to ten rupees, and although he couldn't buy all the things in the rag-seller's shop he wished to, he had been able to buy the jacket, the overcoat, the blanket he slept under, and have a few annas left over for the enjoyment of 'Red-Lamp' cigarettes. His father had been angry at his extravagance, and the boys of the outcastes' colony, even Chota and Ram Charan, cut jokes with him on account of his new rig-out, calling him 'Pilpali sahib' (imitation sahib). And he knew, of course, that except for his English clothes there was nothing English in his life. But he kept up his new form, rigidly adhering to his clothes day and night and guarding them from all base taint of Indianness, not even risking the formlessness of an Indian quilt, though he shivered with the cold at night.

A sharp tremor of cold ran through his hot, massive frame. The hair of his body almost stood on end. He turned on his side and waited in the half-dark for something he knew not what. These nights were awful. So cold and uncomfortable! He liked the days because during the day the sun shone and he could, after he had finished his work, brush his clothes with a rag and walk out into the street, the envy of all his friends and the most conspicuous man in the outcastes' colony. But the nights! 'I must get another blanket,' he said to himself. 'Then father won't ask me to put a quilt on. He always keeps abusing me. I do all his work for him. He appropriates the pay all right. He is afraid of the sepoys. They call him names. He abuses me. He is happy when they call him Jemadar. So proud of his izzat![1] He just goes about getting salaams from everybody. I don't take a moment's rest and yet he abuses me. And if I go to play with the boys he calls me in the middle of the game to come and attend to the latrines. He is old. He doesn't know anything of the sahibs. And now he will call me to get up, and it is *so* cold. He will keep

---

[1]Prestige.

4

lying in bed, and Rakha and Sohini will still be asleep, when I go to the latrines.' He wrinkled his dark, broad, round face with the feeling of pain that came up into his being and made his otherwise handsome features look knotted and ugly. And thus he lay, awaiting his father's call, hating to hear it, yet lying anxiously in expectation of—the rude bullying order to get up.

'Get up, ohe you Bakhya, you son of a pig,' came his father's voice, sure as a bullet to its target, from the midst of a, broken, jarring, interrupted snore. 'Get up and attend to the latrines or the sepoys will be angry.'

The old man seemed to awake instinctively, for a moment, just about that time every morning and then to relapse into his noisy sleep under the greasy, dense, thick, discoloured, patched quilt.

Bakha half opened his eyes and tried to lift his head from the earth as he heard his father's shout. He was angered at the abuse as he was already feeling rather depressed that morning. The high cheek-bones of his face became pallid with sullenness. His mind went back to the morning after his mother's death, when although he, Bakha, was awake, his father had thought he was asleep and presuming he was never going to get up, had shouted at him. That was the beginning of his father's subsequent early-morning calls, which he had begun at first to resist with a casual deafness, and which he now ignored irritatedly. It wasn't that he couldn't get up, because ordinarily he woke up from his slumber quite early, his mother having habituated him to getting up early. She used to give him a brass tankard full of a boiling hot mixture of water, tea-leaves and milk from the steaming earthen saucepan that always lay balanced on the two-bricks-with-a-space-in-between oven or fireplace in a corner of their one-roomed house. It was so delightful, the taste of that hot, sugary liquid, that Bakha's mouth always watered for it on the night before the morning on which he had to drink it. And after he had drunk it he used to put on his clothes and go to work at the latrines, happy and contented. When his mother died and the burden of looking after the family fell on him, there was no time left to look for such comforts and luxuries as an early morning tumblerful of tea. So he learnt to do without it, looking back, however, with fondness to the memory of those days when he lived in the enjoyment not only of the tasty, spicy delights of breakfast, but of all the splendrous details of life, the nice clothes which his mother bought him, the frequent visits to the town and the empty days, filled with play. He often thought of his mother, the small, dark figure, swathed simply in a tunic, a pair of baggy trousers and an apron, crouching as she went about cooking and cleaning the home, a bit too old-fashioned for his then already growing modern tastes, Indian to the core and sometimes uncomfortably so (as she did not like his affecting European clothes), but so loving, so good, and withal generous, giving, always giving, buying him things, kindness personified. He, didn't feel sad, however, to think that she was dead. He just couldn't summon sorrow to the world he lived in, the world of his English clothes and 'Red-Lamp' cigarettes, because it seemed she was not of that world, had no connection with it.

'Are you up? Get up, you illegally begotten came his father's shout again and stirred the boy to a feeling of despair.

'The bully!' Bakha exclaimed under his breath as he listened to the last accents of his father's voice die out in a clumsy, asthmatic cough. He just shook himself and turning his back to his father for sheer cussedness, averted the challenge of the dark, dingy, crowded, little room which seemed to have come with his father's abuse. He felt that his bones were stiff and his flesh numb with the cold. For a moment he felt feverish. A hot liquid trickled down from the corners of his eyes. One of his nostrils seemed to be blocked and he sniffed the air, trying to adjust his breathing to the congested climate of the corner where his face was turned. His throat too seemed to have been caught, for as he inhaled the air it seemed to irritate his trachea uncomfortably. He began to swallow air in order to relieve his nose and his throat. But when a breath of air pierced the cavity which was clogged the other became impenetrable. A cough shook the inner tissues of his throat and he spat furiously into the corner where he lay. He leaned on his elbow and blew his nose under the carpet on which he lay. Then he fell back, his legs gathered together and shrunken under the thin folds of his blanket, his head buried into his arms. He felt very cold. And he dozed off again.

'Oh, Bakhya! Oh, Bakhya! Oh, you scoundrel of a sweeper's son! Come and clear a latrine for me!' someone shouted from without.

Bakha flung the blanket off his body, stretched his legs and arms to shake off the half-sleep that still clung to him, and got up abruptly, yawning and rubbing his eyes. For a moment he bent, rolling the carpet and the blanket to make room for the activity of the day, then, thinking he heard the man outside shout again, he hurried to the door.

A small, thin man, naked except for a loin-cloth, stood outside with a small brass jug in his left hand, a round white cotton skull-cap on his head, a pair of wooden sandals on his feet, and the apron of his loin-cloth lifted to his nose.

It was Havildar Charat Singh, the famous hockey player of the 38th Dogras regiment, as celebrated for his humour as for the fact, which with characteristic Indian openness he acknowledged, that he suffered from chronic piles.

'Why aren't the latrines clean, you rogue of a Bakhe! There is not one fit to go near! I have walked all round! Do you know you are responsible for my piles? I caught the contagion sitting on one of those unclean latrines!'

'All right, Havildar ji, I will get one ready for you at once,' Bakha said cautiously as he proceeded to pick up his brush and basket from the place where these tools decorated the front wall of the house.

He worked away earnestly, quickly, without loss of effort. Brisk, yet steady, his capacity for active application to the task he had in hand seemed to flow like constant water from a natural spring. Each muscle of his body, hard as a rock when it came into play, seemed to shine forth like glass. He must have had immense pent-up resources lying deep, deep in his body, for as he rushed along with considerable skill and alacrity from one doorless latrine to another, cleaning, brushing, pouring phenoil, he seemed as easy as a wave sailing away on a deep-bedded, river. 'What a dexterous workman!' the onlooker would have said. And though his job was dirty he remained comparatively clean. He didn't even soil his sleeves, handling the commodes, sweeping and scrubbing them. 'A bit superior to his job,' they always said, 'not the kind of man who ought to be doing this.' For he looked intelligent, even sensitive, with a sort of dignity that does not belong to the ordinary scavenger, who is as a rule uncouth and unclean. It was perhaps his absorption in his task that gave him the look of distinction, or his exotic dress however loose and ill-fitting, that removed him above his odorous world. Havildar Charat Singh, who had the Hindu instinct for immaculate cleanliness, was puzzled when he emerged from his painful half an hour in the latrines and caught sight of Bakha. Here was a low-caste man who seemed clean! He became rather self-conscious, the prejudice of the 'twice-born[1]' high-caste Hindu against stink, even though he saw not the slightest suspicion of it in Bakha, rising into his mind. He smiled complacently. Then, however, he forgot his high caste and the ironic smile on his face became a childlike laugh.

'You are becoming a gentreman, ohe Bakhya! Where did you get that uniform?

Bakha was shy, knowing he had no right to indulge in such luxuries as apeing the high-caste people. He humbly mumbled:

'Huzoor it is all your blessing.'

Charat Singh was feeling kind, though he did not relax the grin which symbolised six thousand years of racial and class

---

[1]The Brahmins, the Kshatriyas, the two upper caste in Hindu society, justify their superiority by asserting that they have earned their position by the good deeds of multiple lives.

superiority. To express his good-will, however, he said:

'Come this afternoon, Bakhe. I shall give you a hockey stick.' He knew the boy played that game very well.

Bakha stretched himself up; he was astonished yet grateful at Charat Singh's offer. It was a godsend to him, this spontaneous gesture on the part of one of the best hockey players of the regiment. 'A hockey stick! I wonder if it will be a new one!' he thought to himself, and he stood smiling with a queer humility, overcome with gratitude. Charat Singh's generous promise had called forth that trait of servility in Bakha which he had inherited from his forefathers, the weakness, of the down-trodden, the helplessness of the poor and the indigent, suddenly receiving help, the passive contentment of the bottom dog suddenly illuminated by the prospect of fulfilment of a secret and long-cherished desire. He saluted his benefactor and bent down to his work again.

A soft smile lingered on his lips, the smile of a slave overjoyed at the condescension of his master, more akin to pride than to happiness. And he slowly slipped into a song. The steady heave of his body from one latrine to another made the whispered refrain a fairly audible note. And he went forward, with eager step, from job to job, a marvel of movement dancing through his work. Only, the sway of his body was so violent that once the folds of his turban came undone, and the buttons of his overcoat slipped from their worn-out holes. But this did not hinder his work. He clumsily gathered together his loose garments and proceeded with his business.

Men came one after another, towards the latrines. Most of them were Hindus, naked, except for the loin-cloth, brass jugs in hand and with the sacred thread twisted round their left ears. Occasionally came a Mohammedan, who wore a long white cotton tunic and baggy trousers, holding a big copper kettle in his hands.

Bakha broke the tempo of his measured activity to wipe the sweat off his brow with his sleeve. Its woollen texture felt nice and sharp against his skin, but left an irritating warmth behind. It was a pleasant irritation, however, and he went ahead with the renewed vigour that discomfort sometimes gives to the body. 'My work will soon be finished,' he said to himself, seeing that he was almost at the end of one part of his routine. But the end of one job meant to him no escape into the haven of luxury. Not that he shirked work or really liked doing nothing. For, although he didn't know it, to him work was a sort of intoxication which gave him a glowing health and plenty of easy sleep. So he worked on continuously, incessantly, without stopping for breath, even though the violent exertion of his limbs was making him gasp.

At last when he had got to the end of the third row of latrines for the second time during the morning, he felt a cramp in his back and stretched himself out from the bent posture he had maintained all the while. He looked in the direction of the town. There was a slight misty haze before him, a sort of screen which the smouldering fire in the chimney where he had burnt the refuse last night had sent up to mingle with the vaporous fleecy clouds that rose from the surface of the brook. Through the thin film he could see the half-naked brown bodies of the Hindus hurrying to the latrines. Some of those who had already visited the latrines could be seen scrubbing their little brass jugs with clay on the side of the brook. Others were bathing to the tune of 'Ram re Ram,' 'Hari Ram,'—crouching by the water, rubbing their hands, with a little soft earth; washing their feet, their faces; chewing little twigs bitten into the shape of brushes; rinsing their mouths, gargling and spitting noisily into the stream; douching their noses and blowing them furiously, ostentatiously. Ever since he had worked in the British barracks Bakha had been ashamed of the Indian way of performing ablutions, all that gargling and spitting, because he knew the Tommies disliked it. He remembered so well the Tommies' familiar abuse of the natives: '*Kala admi zamin par hagne wala*'(black man, you who relieve yourself on the ground). But he himself had been ashamed at the sight of Tommies running naked to their tub baths. 'Disgraceful,' he had said to himself. They were, however, sahibs. Whatever they did was 'fashun.' But his own countrymen—they were *natus* (natives). He felt amused as an Englishman might be amused, to see a Hindu loosen his dhoti to pour some water first over his navel and then down his back in a flurry of ecstatic hymn-singing. And he watched with contemptuous displeasure the indecent behaviour of a Mohammedan walking about with his hands buried deep in his trousers, purifying himself in the ritual manner, preparatory to his visit to the mosque. 'I wonder what they say in their prayers?' he asked himself. 'Why do they sit, stand, bend and kneel as if they were doing exercises?' Once, he remembered, he had asked Ali, the son of a regimental bandsman, why they did that, but Ali would not tell him and was angry, saying that Bakha was insulting his religion. And he recalled the familiar sight of all those naked Hindu men and women who could be seen squatting in the open, outside the city, every morning. 'So shameless,' he thought; 'they don't seem to care who looks at them, sitting there like that. It is on account of that that the goras white men call them *kala log zamin par hagne wala* (black man, you who relieve yourself on the ground). Why don't they come here?' But then he realised that if they came to the latrines his work would increase and he didn't relish the idea. He preferred to imagine himself sweeping the streets in the place of his father. '*That* is easy work,' he said to himself, 'I will only have to lift cow-dung and horse-dung with a shovel and sweep the dust of the road with a broom.'

'There is not a latrine clean. You must work for the pay you receive.'

Bakha turned abruptly and noticed Ramanand the peevish old black moneylender shouting at him in his sharp southern diction. He bowed with joined hands to Ramanand who was staring at him, a pair of gold rings studded with rubies in his ears, a transparent muslin loin-cloth and shirt on his portentous belly, and a funny string cap of a turban on his head. 'Maharaj,' he said and ran towards the latrines and busied himself with his job again.

He hardly realised that he had lapsed into activity, so vigorously did he attack his job. And he was completely oblivious during the quarter of an hour he took to finish a fourth round of the latrines, oblivious alike of the time and of the sweat trickling down his forehead, of the warmth in his body and of the sense of power that he felt as he ended up.

The spurts of smoke from the chimney near his house made him conscious of the next job he had to attend to. He went towards it half-heartedly, and after pausing for a while to pick up a trident-shaped shovel, began to stuff the aperture of the little brick pyramid with the straw in the baskets which he had collected from the latrines.

Little pieces of straw flew into the air as he shovelled the refuse into the chimney, the littlest pieces settling on his clothes, the slightly bigger ones settling on the ground where he had to collect them again with his broom. But he worked unconsciously. This forgetfulness or emptiness persisted in him over long periods. It was a sort of insensitivity created in him by the kind of work he had to do, a tough skin which must be a shield against all the most awful sensations. Stooping down over the baskets full of straw, he gathered shovelfuls and cast them into the grate till it seemed congested and it would take no more. Then he picked up a long poker and prodded the fire. Quickly it flared up, suddenly illuminating the furnace with its leaping red, gold and black flames, an angry consuming power, something apart, something detached from the heaps of straw it fed on.

The blood in Bakha's veins tingled with the heat as he stood before it. His dark face, round and solid and exquisitely well defined, lit with a queer sort of beauty. The toil of the body had built up for him a very fine physique. It seemed to suit him, to give a homogeneity, a wonderful wholeness to his body, so that you could turn round and say: 'Here is a man.' And it seemed to give him a nobility, strangely in contrast with his filthy profession and with the sub-human status to which he was condemned from birth.

This was a long task, lasting almost twenty minutes. Bakha, however, did not seem to feel the strain of it as he had felt the strain of his earlier occupation. The burning flame seemed to ally itself with him. It seemed to give him a sense of power, the power to destroy. It seemed to infuse into him a masterful instinct somewhat akin to sacrifice. It seemed as if burning or destruction was for him a form of physical culture.

When the chimney had consumed the last basket of straw and refuse Bakha closed its mouth and retreated. He felt thirsty. The edges of his lips were dry, He put back the shovel, the basket, the broom and the brushes in their place. Then he moved towards the door of his hut, sniffing the air full of smoke from the chimney, brushing his clothes and smoothing them out. His thirst became overpowering as he entered the room. Looking dazedly at the utensils lying about in a corner, he felt he wanted tea. But as he surveyed the room he heard his father still snoring under his patched quilt. His brother was not in the room. He knew at once where he would be—playing in the maidan by the street. As he stood staring round in order to get used to the comparative darkness, he saw that his sister was trying to light a fire between two bricks. She was blowing hard at it, lifting herself on her haunches as she crouched on the mud floor. Her head almost touched the ground, but each puff from her mouth succeeded only in raising a spurt of smoke and was beaten back by the wet wooden sticks that served as fuel. She sat back helpless when she heard her brother's footsteps. Her smoke-irritated eyes were full of water. She turned and saw her brother. Real tears began to flow down her cheeks.

'Will you get up and let me blow at it?' Bakha said. And without waiting for a reply he walked up to the corner of the room, sat down on his knees, shook the fuel and stooping, began to blow. His big, round mouth seemed like a real bellows as it sent the breath whirring into the fireplace and started first a few sparks, then a blazing fire through the damp sticks. He put the earthen pan over the little stove.

'There is no water in that,' his sister said.

'I will get some water from the pitcher,' he said, as he casually made towards the corner.

'There is no water in the pitcher either,' she answered.

'Oh!' he exclaimed under his breath, tired and exasperated. And for a moment he stood defeated where he had bent down to the pitcher.

'I shall go and get some water,' said Sohini meekly.

'All right,' agreed Bakha without any show of formality, and going out of doors sat down on the edge of a broken cane chair, the only article of furniture of European design which he had been able to acquire in pursuance of his ambition to live like an Englishman. Sohini picked up the pitcher, poised it easily on her head, and ran past her brother.

How a round base can be adjusted on a round top, how a sphere can rest on a sphere is a problem which may be of interest to those who think like Euclid or Archimedes. It never occurred to Sohini to ask herself anything like this as she balanced her pitcher on her head and went to and from her one-roomed home to the steps of the caste-well where she counted on the chance of some gentleman taking pity on her and giving her the water she needed. She had a sylph-like form, not thin but full-bodied within the limits of her graceful frame, well rounded on the hips, with an arched narrow waist from which descended the folds of her trousers and above which were her full, round, globular breasts, jerking slightly, for lack of a bodice, under her transparent muslin shirt. Bakha observed her as she walked along swaying. She was beautiful. He was proud of her with a pride not altogether that of a brother for a sister.

The outcastes were not allowed to mount the platform surrounding the well, because if they were ever to draw water from it, the Hindus of the three upper castes would consider the water polluted. Nor were they allowed access to the near-by brook as their use of it would contaminate the stream. They had

14

no well of their own because it cost at least a thousand rupees to dig a well in such a hilly town as Bulashah. Perforce they had to collect at the foot of the caste Hindus' well and depend on the bounty of some of their superiors to pour water into their pitchers. More often than not there was no caste Hindu present. They were all rich enough to get the water-carriers to supply them with plenty of fresh water every morning for their baths and kitchens, and only those came to the well who were either fond of an open-air bath or too poor to pay for the water-carriers' services. So the outcastes had to wait for chance to bring some caste Hindu to the well, for luck to decide that he was kind, for Fate to ordain that he had time—to get their pitchers filled with water. They crowded round the well, congested the space below its high brick platform, morning, noon and night, joining their hands with servile humility to every passer-by, cursing their fate, and bemoaning their lot, if they were refused the help they wanted, praying, beseeching and blessing, if some generous soul condescended to listen to them, or to help them.

When Sohini reached the well there were already about ten other outcastes waiting. But there was no one to give them water. She had come as fast as she could to the well, full of fear and anxiety that she would have to wait her turn since she could see from a distance that there was already a crowd. She didn't feel disappointed so much as depressed to realise that she would be the tenth to receive water. She had sensed with her deep woman's instinct the feeling in her brother's soul. He was tired. He was thirsty. She had felt like a mother as she issued from her home to fetch water, a mother going out to fetch food or drink for her loved ones at home. Now as she sat in a row with her fellow-sufferers, her heart sank. There was no sign of any-one passing that way who could be a possible benefactor. But she was patient. She had in her an instinctive fortitude, obvious in her curious reserve, in her composed and peaceful bearing.

Gulabo, the washerwoman, the mother of Ram Charan, her brother's friend, had observed Sohini approach. She was a fair-complexioned, middle-aged woman, the regularity of whose supple body bore even in its decay the evidence of a form which must, in her youth, have been wonderful. But although her face was now covered with wrinkles she had pretensions to beauty and was notorious as an assertive old hussy who thought herself superior to every other outcaste, first because she claimed a high place in the hierarchy of the castes among the low castes, secondly, because a well-known Hindu gentleman in the town who had been her lover in her youth was still kind to her in her middle age.

Now Sohini being of the lowest caste among the outcastes would naturally be looked down upon by Gulabo. The delicate features of her rising beauty had added fuel to Gulabo's fire. The girl was a potential rival. Gulabo hated the very sight of her innocent, honest face, though she would not confess, even to herself, that she was jealous of the sweeper girl. But she unconsciously betrayed her feeling in the mockery and light-hearted abuse which she showered on Sohini. The consciousness of that prettiness which people's compliments stimulated in her, made the young woman vaguely surmise it all.

'Go back home,' said Gulabo mockingly. 'There is no one to give you water here! And, at any rate, there are so many of us ahead of you!'

Sohini smiled evasively, then recognising an elderly man in the company, she modestly drew her apron from her head a little over her eyes. And she sat still, crouching by her pitcher.

'Have you heard of such immodesty!' exclaimed Gulabo to Waziro, the weaver's wife who sat near her. 'This sweeper girl goes about without an apron over her head all day in town and in the cantonment.'

'Really!' exclaimed Waziro, pretending to be shocked though she knew Gulabo's evil tongue and had nothing against Sohini. 'You ought to be ashamed of yourself,' she said, winking an aside to the girl.

Sohini could not suppress her amusement at so comic an

assurance of friendliness as Waziro's and laughed.

'Think of it! Think of it! You bitch! You prostitute! wanton! And your mother hardly dead. Think of laughing in my face, laughing at me who am old enough to be your mother. Bitch!' the washerwoman exploded.

Sohini laughed still more hilariously at the ridiculous abruptness of Gulabo's abuse.

'Ari, you bitch! Do you take me for a buffoon? What are you laughing at, slut? Aren't you ashamed of showing your teeth to me in the presence of men, you prostitute?' shouted Gulabo, and she looked towards the old man and the little boys who were of the company.

Sohini now realised that the woman was angry. 'But I haven't done anything to annoy her,' she reflected. 'She herself began it all and is abusing me right and left. I didn't pick the quarrel. I have more cause to be angry than she has!'

'Bitch, why don't you speak! Prostitute, why don't you answer me?' Gulabo insisted.

'Please don't abuse me,' the girl said, 'I haven't said anything to you.'

'You annoy me with your silence, you illegally begotten! You eater of dung and drinker of urine! You bitch of a sweeper women! I will show you how to insult one old enough to be your mother.' And she rose with upraised arm and rushed at Sohini.

Waziro, the weaver's wife, ran after her and caught her just before she had time to hit the sweeper girl.

'Be calm, be calm; you must not do that,' she said as she dragged Gulabo back to her seat. 'No, you must not do that.'

A flutter of excitement travelled through the little group, exclamations, shouts and cries of 'Hai, Hai,' and strange looks of disgust, indignation and disapproval were exchanged. Sohini was a bit frightened at first and grew pale, but she kept intensely still and avoiding the shock, subsided into a listless apathy. As she looked away, however, and cast her eyes up to the blue heavens overhead, she felt a sort of dreariness, a pain, which, though she accepted it resignedly, brought a hurtfulness with it. Sad and wistful, she heaved a soft sigh and felt something in her heart asking for mercy. The sun overhead shot down bright arrows of heat, and inspired a feeling of the passing of time, a feeling that made her forget the unsolicited quarrel with Gulabo, but cast over her the miserable, soul-harrowing shadow of the vision of her brother waiting for her at home, thirsty after the morning's toil, dying for a cup of tea. And yet no caste Hindu seemed to be near.

Minutes passed in silence, only slightly disturbed by Gulabo's sobs and sighs. 'On the day of my little daughter's marriage too! This inauspicious sweeper woman has started my auspicious day so badly!' she was saying. But no one heeded her. And then at long last, a belated caste Hindu visitor to the latrines was passing. He was a sepoy from the neighbouring regiment.

'Oh, Maharaj! Maharaj! Won't you draw us some water, please? We beg you. We have been waiting here a long time, we will be grateful,' shouted the chorus of voices as they pressed towards him, some standing up, bending and joining their palms in beggary, others twisting their lips in various attitudes of servile appeal and abject humility as they remained seated.

Either the sepoy was a callous brute or in too much of a hurry. But he passed by without heeding the request of the group collected at the foot of the well.

Luckily for the crowd of outcastes, however, there was another man coming a little way behind, no less a person than Pundit Kali Nath, one of the priests in charge of the temple in the town. The crowd repeated their entreaties with more vehemence than before.

The Pundit hesitated, twitched his eyebrows and looked at the group frowning with the whole of his bony, hollow-cheeked, deeply-furrowed face. The appeal seemed, even to his dry-as-dust self, irresistible. But he was an ill-humoured old devil, and had it not been that, as he stood and reflected, he realised that the exercise at the well might do some good to the chronic constipation from which he suffered, he would not have consented to help the outcastes.

He moved slowly on to the brick platform of the well. His small, cautious steps and the peculiar contortions of his face showed that he was a prey to a morbid preoccupation with his inside. He took his own time to prepare for the task he had undertaken. He seemed to be immersed in thought, but was really engrossed in the rumblings in his belly. 'That rice,' he thought, 'the rice I ate yesterday, that must be responsible. My stomach seems jammed. Or was it the sweet jalebis I ate with my milk at the confectioner's? But the food at the home of Lalla Banarsi Das may have introduced complications.' He recalled the taste of the various delicacies to which he was so often treated by the pious. 'How nice and sweet is the milk-rice pudding, sticking to the white teeth and lingering in the mouth. And kara parshad, the semolina pudding; the hot, buttery masses of it melt almost as you put a morsel of it in the mouth. But the hubble-bubble usually keeps my stomach clean. What happened to this morning's smoke? I smoked for an hour to no effect. Strange!' During the time taken by these cogitations he had placed the brass jug in his hand to rest in a little hollow in the wooden frame of the well. The waiting crowd thought that it was the Brahmin's disgust at serving them, the outcastes, that brought such deep wrinkles on his face and made it look peeved and angry. They didn't realise that it was constipation and a want of vigour in his lanky little limbs. They soon realised this, for as, after a great many hesitant steps, he tied the iron can that lay near the frame to an edge of the hemp rope that skirted the pulley-wheel, and gently lowered it into the well, the handle slipped from his hand, because of the weight of the bucket, and revolved violently back, releasing all the coils of rope that were around it. He was a bit scared by the suddenness of the motion of the wheel. Then he pulled himself together and renewed his attack. But he was soon upset again. To draw out a can, full of water, required limbs which had been used to exercise more strenuous than the Pundit had ever performed, his whole life revolving round endless recitation of sacred verses and the writing of an occasional charm or horoscope with a reed pen. He exerted all his strength and strained to roll the handle on. His face was contorted, but not altogether unlit with pleasure, because already the exercise of his muscles made him feel much easier in the belly than he had done for days. The expectant outcastes were busy getting their pitchers ready, but as that only meant shifting themselves into position so to be nearest to this most bountiful, most generous of men, all their attention was fixed on him. And as that disclosed the apparent effort the athlete was making, they exerted all their energies, all their will-power to aid him in his task.

At length the can was on the brick platform. But the Brahmin becoming interested in the stirrings of his stomach, in the changing phases of his belly, looked, for a moment, absent-minded. A subtle wave of warmth seemed to have descended slowly down from his arms to the pit of his abdomen, and he felt a strange stirring above his navel such as he had not experienced for months, so pleasing was it in its intimations of the relief it would bring him. Then, unfortunately, a sharp pain shot through like a pin-prick on the right-hand side of his waist and his demeanour assumed the anxious, agitated look habitual to it.

'I am first, Pundit ji,' said Gulabo the washerwoman impetuously, and suddenly disturbed the Brahmin who was absorbed in himself.

He frowned at her and not noticing the vamping expression she had assumed, deprived her of the favourable attention that would have been her due if he had.

'No, I came first,' shouted an inconspicuous little boy.

'But you know that I was here before you,' shouted someone else.

And there was a general stampede towards the well that would, in ordinary circumstances, have flurried the priest into throwing water on all of them. But he had as good an eye for a pretty face as he had an ear for the sound of a request. Sohini had sat patiently away from the throng, the while it charged the well. The Pundit recognised her as the sweeper's daughter. He had seen her before, noticed her as she came to clean the latrines in the gullies in the town—the fresh young form whose full breasts with their dark beads of nipples stood out so conspicuously under her muslin shirt, whose innocent look of wonder seemed to stir the only soft chord in his person, hardened by the congenital weakness of his body, disillusioned by the congenital weakness of his mind, brazened by the authority he exercised over the faithful and the devout. And he was inclined to be kind to her.

'Oh, you Lakha's daughter, come here,' he said, 'you have been patient and the reward of patience, say the holy books, is supreme. Get away, you noisy curs, get out of the way!'

'But Pundit ji!' said Sohini, hesitating to receive the favour, not because she divined the Brahmin's admiration, but because she was afraid of all those who had come before her.

'Now come along,' urged the Pundit, irritated by the beginning in his belly of the urge for excretion, and exhilarated by the thought of doing the beautiful girl a favour. The girl advanced meekly and put her pitcher down under the platform. The priest lifted the can with a great effort. For a moment he successfully handled the water, being surcharged with the glow of that warmth which he felt being near Sohini, intoxicated by it. Then his normal weakness returned. So he splashed the water and the outcastes flew on all sides, half wet, half dry.

'Get out of the way!' he shouted as he poured the water into Sohini's pitcher. He was attempting to cover his weakness by bullying. At length the pitcher was three-quarters full.

'Have you got enough now?' asked the Pundit in triumph as he withdrew the empty can.

'Yes, Pundit ji,' Sohini whispered, her head bent in modesty, as she wiped the outside of the pitcher to lift it on to her head.

'Look, why don't you come and clean the courtyard of our house at the temple,' called the Brahmin as the girl withdrew.

21

'Tell your father to send you from to-day.' And he looked long at her, rather embarrassed, his rigid respectability fighting against the waves of amorousness that had begun to flow in his blood.

'You will come to-day,' he firmly said lest there should be any misunderstanding left in her mind about it.

Sohini was grateful for the favour he had shown her. She shyly nodded and went her way, her left hand on her waist, her right on the pitcher and a balance in her steps like the rhythm of a song. The washerwoman cast dark and angry glances at her as she herself sullenly drew nearer the well with the rest of the crowd which had now begun to appeal to a new-comer for help.

This was Lachman, a Hindu water-carrier, a Brahmin who in spite of his mean occupation was allowed to go and wash the utensils of the caste Hindus, to cook their food, to fetch their water, and to do other odd jobs about their houses. He was a young man, about twenty-six, with the intelligent though rather rugged features of the Brahmin who has come down in status. A bamboo pole to the extreme ends of which were adjusted four strings (supporting wooden brackets to carry pitchers) was on his shoulders. He rested it slowly on the ground and ascending the well, joined his hands in greeting to the Pundit, saying, 'Jay deva,' Long live the Gods, and respectfully relieved him of the job of drawing more water from the well. As he threw the can easily into the well, however, he looked sideways towards Sohini who was retreating home. He too had noticed her before and felt a stirring in his blood, the warm impulse of love, the strangely affecting desire of the soul to reach out to something beyond, at first in fear, then in hope and then with all the concentrated fury of a bodily and mental obsession. Sometimes he had playfully irritated her with mild jokes, when she came to the well and he happened to be there. She had responded with a modest smile and a subtle look of her shining, lustrous eyes. And he was, as he said, in the language characteristic of the Indian lover, 'dead over her.' The Pundit caught him in the act of looking back. Shame-faced. Lachman withdrew his gaze, and with that servility which he shared with the other menials, quietly turned to the job he had in hand. Soon the strength of his arm had brought the can full of water to the top of the well. He first filled the Pundit's little brass jug and Gulabo's pitcher, and then set about to help the others. The picture of Sohini disappeared from his mind.

She, however, figured conspicuously in the corner of the little mud-house which was her kitchen. Her father was abusing her, as he now sat on his bed, puff-puffing away at the cane tube of his hubble-bubble though he was still wrapped in his patched quilt.

'I thought you were dead or something, you daughter of a pig!' Lakha was shouting. 'No tea, no piece of bread, and I am dying of hunger! Put the tea on and call those sons of a pig, Bakha and Rakha, to me!' Then he frowned in the gruff manner of a man who was really good and kind at heart, but who knew he was weak and infirm and so bullied his children, to preserve his authority, lest he should be repudiated by them, refused and rejected as the difficult old rubbish he was.

Sohini obeyed him at once, shouting for her brothers as she put the earthen saucepan on the fire.

'Vay Bakhia, vay Rakhia, father is calling you!'

Bakha alone came into the room in answer to his sister's call, Rakha having slipped away to play, early in the morning.

The boy was wiping the sweat off his face and neck and breathing hard, for he had been to do another round at the latrines. His black eyes shed fire and his big, broad face was slightly contracted with fatigue. His throat was parched and dry.

I have a pain in my side,' said the old man to his son, as the boy came in and stood towering in the doorway, the whites of his eyes glaring. 'You go and sweep the temple courtyard and the main road for me, and call that swine of a Rakha, wherever he is, to come and attend to the latrines here.'

'Father, the Pundit of the temple wanted me to clean the family house at the temple,' said Sohini.

'Well then go and do so! *why do you eat my head?*' snapped Lakha peevishly.

'Is your pain very bad? asked Bakha ironically, to make his father conscious of his bad temper. 'I will rub your side with oil if you like.'

'No, no,' said the old man irritably, turning his face to hide the shame which his son's subtle protest aroused in him. He had no pain at all in his side, or anywhere, and was merely foxing, being in his old age, ineffectual, and excusing himself from work like a child. 'No, no,' he said, 'you go and attend to the work. I'll be all right.' And he smiled gently.

Meanwhile the mixture of tea-leaves, water, milk and sugar was ready. Sohini poured some of it into two earthen bowls, glazed on the inside. Bakha came, and lifting one, gave it to his father. Then he picked up the other and put it to his lips in hot haste. The sharp, warm taste of the liquid sent forth a queer delight spreading into his flesh. His tongue was slightly burnt with the small sips because he did not, as his father did, blow on the tea to cool it. This was another of the things he had learnt at the British barracks from the Tommies. His uncle had said that the goras didn't enjoy the full flavour of the tea because they did not blow on it. But Bakha considered that both his uncle's and his father's spattering sips were natu habits. He would have told his father that the sahibs didn't do that. But he was too respectful by habit to suggest such a thing, although, of course, for himself he accepted the custom of the English Tommies and followed it implicitly. After he had drunk his tea and eaten a piece of bread from the basket which Sohini put before her father, Bakha went out. He picked up the big broom of thin, very thin cane sticks with a stump of a wooden handle, and the basket with which his father used to go out sweeping the roads. Then he, walked away towards the town, realising, for the first time, the strange coincidence of his morning's wish with his father's sudden injunction.

The lane leading to the outcastes' street was soon left behind.

It seemed such a short lane to him to-day. Where the lane finished, the heat of the sun seemed to spread as from a bonfire out into the empty space of the grounds beyond the outcastes' colony. He sniffed at the clean, fresh air around the flat stretch of land before him and vaguely sensed a difference between the odorous, smoky world of refuse and the open, radiant world of the sun. He wanted to warm his flesh; he wanted the warmth to get behind the scales of the dry, powdery surface that had formed on his fingers; he wanted the blood in the blue veins that stood out on the back of his hand to melt. He turned his hands so as to show them to the sun. He lifted his face to the sun, open-eyed for a moment, then with the pupils of his eyes half closed, half open. And he lifted his chin upright. It was pleasing to him. It seemed to give him a thrill, a queer sensation which spread on the surface of his flesh where the tincture of warmth penetrated the numbed skin. He felt vigorous in this bracing atmosphere. Instinctively he rubbed his face in order to make it warm enough to take in the rays of the sun, to open out its pores. So he adjusted the broom and the basket under his arms and caressed his face with the palms of his hands. A couple of brisk rubs and he felt the blood in his cheeks rising to the high bones under the shadow of his eyes and into the ears which shone red-tipped and transparent at the sides of his head. He felt as he used to do when, on winter Sundays in his childhood, he used to strip himself naked, except for a loincloth, to stand in the sun, and rub mustard oil on his body. Recollecting this he looked up at the sun. He caught the full force of its glare, and was dazed. He stood lost for a moment, confused in the shimmering rays, feeling as though there were nothing but the sun, the sun, the sun, everywhere, in him, on him, before him and behind him. It was a pleasant sensation in spite of the disconcerting suddenness with which it had engulfed him. He felt suspended, as it were, in a region of buoyant tenseness.

As he emerged from the world of that rare, translucent lustre into which he had been lifted, he stumbled over a stone and muttered a curse. Looking ahead he saw that he was being observed by Ram Charan, the washerman's son, by Chota, the leather-worker's son, and his own brother, Rakha. He felt abashed at being seen absorbed in talking to himself. They always made a butt of him, ridiculing the weight of his body, the shape of his clothes, his gait, which was a bit like an elephant's, on account of his heavy, swaying buttocks, and a bit like a tiger's, lithe and supple. He thought they would mock at him if they saw him massaging his face or talking to himself, especially as he knew they knew that he was a devotee of 'fashun,' a weakness which they shared with him and yet for which they ridiculed him. Bakha would always retaliate by pointing at the washer-boy's lashless, browless eyes and saying: 'That comes of using too much soap to whiten your skin.' And there were other peculiarities about Ram Charan, the fact that he had Gulabo for a mother, and a rather pretty flirtatious sister, the fact that he was a very bony, thin little figure, and drove an ass, blind of one eye, to the waterside, which made the basis of a good joke. Chota he could not attack, for that regular-featured lad was the smartest fellow about the lane, with his neatly oiled hair, khaki shorts and white tennis shoes. Almost a model 'gentreman' Bakha thought him, the kind of person he admired and wanted to follow. With him, therefore, he had an intimate understanding which made the jokes they cut about each other always more tolerable.

'Come, o bey brother-in-law,' greeted Ram Charan, blinking his lashless eyes and looking up.

'I want to be your brother-in-law if you will let me', said Bakha, turning the washer-boy's light abuse into a mild joke based on the fact that he was known to everyone to be an admirer of Ram Charan's sister.

'Well, she is being married to-day, so you are too late,' replied Ram Charan, pleased to contemplate that Bakha would never be able to make the same joke again.

'Oh, is that why you are wearing such nice clothes to-day!' remarked Bakha. 'I see! What a fine waistcoat that! Only a bit

frayed, that gold thread on the velvet. Why don't you iron it?
And oh, I like that chain! By the way, is there a watch attached
to it or is it merely for "fashun"?' Ram Charan flushed red and
subsided. Chota sat quietly smiling at the interchange. Rakha was
apparently feeling cold from the way he had made muffs for his
hands of the long sleeves of the torn and battered overcoat he had
inherited from Bakha and from the manner in which he was
hugging his arms close to his chest. A few other outcastes were
busy killing lice from the pleats of their shirts and trousers and
too comfortable in the sun to bother to look up. As they sat or
stood in the sun, showing their dark hands and feet, they had a
curiously lackadaisical, lazy, lousy look about them. It seemed
their insides were concentrated in the act of emergence, of a new
birth, as it were, from the raw, bleak wintry feeling in their souls
to the world of warmth. The taint of the dark, narrow, dingy little
prison cells of their one-roomed homes lurked in them, however,
even in the outdoor air. They were silent as if the act of liberation
was too much for them to bear. The great life-giver had cut the
inscrutable knots that tied them up in themselves. It had melted
the innermost parts of their being. And their souls stared at the
wonder of it all, the mystery of it, the miracle of it.

It was some time before they nodded a greeting to Bakha.
But he understood them like that. For though he considered them
his inferiors since he came back with sharpened wits from the
British barracks, he still recognised them as his neighbours, the
intimates with whose lives, whose thoughts, whose feelings he
had to make a compromise. He didn't expect them to be formal.
And as he stood for a while among them, he became a part of
the strange, brooding, mysterious crowd that was seeking the
warmth of the sun. One didn't need to employ a courtesy, a
greeting to become part of this gathering as one does in the world
where there is plenty of light and happiness. For in the lives of
this riff-raff, this scum of the earth, these dregs of humanity,
only silence, grim silence, the silence of death fighting for life,
prevailed.

Once Bakha was with them, however, his own and their queer reactions to the beauty of the morning emerged.

'Why, O Bakhe,' said Chota, beaming with the happiness of the sun of which he seemed a favoured child as the light played on his dark, greasy face: 'Where are you off to-day?'

'My father is ill,' replied Bakha, 'so I am going to sweep the roads in the town and the temple courtyard in his stead.' Then he turned to his brother and said: 'Oh, Rakhia, why did you run away early in the morning? Father is ill and there is all the work at the latrines to do in my absence. Come, my brother, run back home. Sohini has kept some hot tea for you, too.'

Rakha, a short, long-faced, black, stumpy little man, seemed to resent his brother's reprimand. But he quickly got up and sullenly faced the path leading homewards.

'Don't you go! Don't go!' called Ram Charan naughtily after him. This, your brother, wants to be a 'gentreman' and to work on the roads while he wants you to do the dirty work at the latrines.'

'Don't buk buk, o bey brother-in-law,' said Bakha good-humouredly. 'Let him go and work for a bit.'

'Come and play khuti!' said Chota, turning to a packet of 'Red-Lamp' cigarettes he had fished out of a shirt pocket, to see how many it contained before offering one to Bakha. 'Come,' he said, 'we will go and join the others.' He referred to Clayton, a black-skinned bandsman, and Godu, the carpenter's son, who were playing marbles round a hole in the ground.

'Come,' urged Chota, 'we shall win some money.'

'No, I must go to my work,' Bakha said, sternly declining the suggestion. 'My father might see me and he will be angry.'

'Forget the old man, come for a while,' Chota insisted persuasively.

'Come, come,' seduced Ram Charan.

They were truants and expected the call of their parents any time. But they believed in dangerous living and had never missed a morning's sun, however much they were rebuked at home, or even beaten. Bakha had principles. With him duty came first, although he was a champion at all kinds of games and would have beaten them hollow at khuti. He seemed intent on his work and he was going to move on.

'All right, wait,' said Chota. 'There, I see the son of the burra babu coming. What about hockey to-day? The boys of the 31st Punjabis sent a "challenge" to play a match against us.'

'I shall come if my father allows me,' said Bakha. Then he looked aside and seeing two white-clad, delicate young boys, greeted them by raising his right hand to his forehead.

'Salaam, babu ji,' he said respectfully.

The elder of the two boys, a simple, innocent, rather plain child of ten, angular, bony, with a flat nose and prominent cheekbones, smiled back kindly. There was a twinkle of recognition in the dark eyes of the little one, about eight years of age, with a mischievous egg-shaped face, alive in every feature from his big forehead to his pouting, thick lower lip and his determined little chin.

'Come, you boys!' greeted Ram Charan and Chota with an impudent swagger. 'What about hockey to-day? There is a match with the boys of the 31st Punjabis.'

'We shall play in the afternoon,' said the little one enthusiastically jumping where he stood, holding his brother's finger. He was hardly big enough to hold a stick and he ignored the fact that he hadn't been asked, because he knew the boys never allowed him to play, saying he was too small and that they were afraid he would get hurt and would go and tell on them.

'All right, will you give us the sticks?' asked Ram Charan, cunningly taking advantage of the child's enthusiasm to exact a promise which, though it was more likely to be repudiated than kept, might serve as a precaution against the child's obstinacy if that mood came upon him that afternoon, as it often did when he was not asked to play.

The sons of the babu, being influential with the captain of the regimental hockey team, because of the exalted position of their father, had had a dozen or so discarded hockey sticks given to them. The boys of the neighbourhood who composed the 38th Dogras boys' eleven, were mostly the poor sons of the Untouchables, dependent on the bounty of the babus' sons for the loan of a stick every afternoon for a practice game. The elder of the two was always a very obliging boy. He willingly suffered his mother's abuse for playing with the outcastes. But the younger one had to be humoured before he would yield.

'Yes, I have brought a nice new stick from Havildar Charat Singh,' he said, 'and a new ball.' Then all of a sudden he turned peevishly to his brother, nudged him and exclaimed: 'Come, don't you want to go to school! We will be late!'

Bakha noticed the ardent, enthusiastic look that lighted up the little one's face. The anxiety of going to school! How beautiful it felt! How nice it must be to be able to read and write! One could read the papers after having been to school. One could talk to the sahibs. One wouldn't have to run to the scribe every time a letter came. And one wouldn't have to pay him to have one's letters written. He had often felt like reading Waris Shah's *Hir and Ranjah*.[1] And he had felt a burning desire, while he was in the British barracks, to speak the *tish-mish, tish-mish* which the Tommies spoke.

His uncle at the British barracks had told him when he first expressed the wish to be a sahib that he would have to go to school if he wanted to be one. And he had wept and cried to be allowed to go to school. But then his father had told him that schools were meant for the babus, not for the lowly sweepers. He hadn't quite understood the reason for that then. Later at the British barracks he realised why his father had not sent him to school.. He was a sweeper's son and could never be a babu. Later still he realised that there was no school which would admit him because the parents of the other children would not allow their sons to be contaminated by the touch of the low-caste man's

---

[1] An epic poem of the Punjab.

sons. How absurd, he thought, that was, since most of the Hindu children touched him willingly at hockey and wouldn't mind having him at school with them. But the masters woaldn't teach the outcastes, lest their fingers which guided the students across the text should touch the leaves of the outcastes' books and they be polluted. These old Hindus were cruel. He was a sweeper, he knew, but he could not consciously accept that fact. He had begun to work at the latrines at the age of six and resigned himself to the hereditary life of the craft, but he dreamed of becoming a sahib. Several times he had felt the impulse to study on his own. Life at the Tommies' barracks had fired his imagination. And he often sat in his spare time and tried to feel how it felt to read. Recently he had actually gone and bought a first primer of English. But his self-education hadn't proceeded beyond the alphabet. To-day as he stood in the sun looking at the eager little boy dragging his brother to school, a sudden impulse came on him to ask the babu's son to teach him.

'Babu ji,' he said, addressing the elder boy, 'in what class are you now?'

'In the fifth class,' the boy answered.

'Surely now you know enough to teach.'

'Yes,' the boy replied.

'Then, do you think it will be too much trouble for you to give me a lesson a day?' Seeing the boy hesitate, he added: 'I shall pay you for it.'

He spoke in a faint, faltering voice, and his humility increased in depth and sincerity with every syllable.

The babu's sons didn't get much pocket-money. Their parents were thrifty and considered, perhaps rightly, that a child should not eat irregularly, as the low-caste boys did, buying things in the bazaar. The elder boy had developed a strong materialistic instinct, hoarding the stray pice or two he received from anyone.

'Very well,' he said. 'I will. But the . . .' He wanted to change the topic, to make his suppressed desire for money less

31

obvious. Bakha knew from his glance what he meant.

'I will pay you an anna per lesson.'

The babu's son smiled a hypocritical smile which seemed queer in so young a person. And he signified his assent, adding as an afterthought the conventional moneylover's phrase: 'Oh, the money doesn't matter.'

'Shall we begin this afternoon?' pleaded Bakha.

'Yes,' the boy agreed, and was inclined to stand to talk and cement the bond with pleasant words, but his brother was now very peevish and tugged at his sleeve, not only because he thought they were late for school, but also because he hated the idea of his brother becoming rich, was jealous of the money he would be earning.

'Come,' shouted the little one, 'the sun is almost overhead! We will be beaten for being late at school.'

Bakha divined the nature of the child's anger and tried to placate him by offering a bribe.

'You will also teach me, won't you, little brother? I will give you a pice a day.'

Bakha knew this would appease the boy's jealousy and obviate any chance of his telling upon his elder brother for spite. He knew if the little one told his.mother that his elder brother was teaching a sweeper to read, she would fly into a rage and turn the poor boy out of the house. He knew her to be a pious Hindu lady.

The little one was too flurried to appreciate the value of the bribe. He looked towards school and was obsessed by the lateness of the hour. He pulled at the lower edge of his brother's tunic and dragged him away.

Bakha saw them depart. He felt elated at the prospect of the lesson he was to take in the afternoon and proceeded to go.

'Stop, O *Babu*! Now you are going to be a very big man,' shouted Ram Charan ironically. 'You won't even talk to us.'

'You are mad,' answered Bakha jovially. 'I must go, the sun is "coming on". And I have to clean the temple approach, and the courtyard.'

'All right, let me show you my madness at hockey to-day.'

'Very well,' Bakha said as he headed towards the gates of the town, his basket under one arm, his broom under the other, and in his heart a song as happy as the lark's.

Tan-nana-nan-tan, rang the bells of a bullock-cart behind him as, like other pedestrians, he was walking in the middle of the road. He jumped aside, dragging his boots in the dust, where, thanks to the inefficiency of the Municipal Committee, the pavement should have been but was not. The fine particles of dust that flew to his face as he walked and the creaking of the cart-wheels in the deep ruts seemed to give him an intense pleasure. Near the gates of the town were a number of stalls at which fuel was sold to those who came to burn their dead in the cremation ground a little way off. A funeral procession had stopped at one of these. They were carrying a corpse on an open stretcher. The body lay swathed in a red cloth painted with golden stars. Bakha stared at it and felt for a moment the grim fear of death, a fear akin to the terror of meeting a snake or a thief. Then he assured himself by thinking: 'Mother said, it is lucky to see a dead body when one is out in the streets.' And he walked on, past the little fruit-stalls where dirtily clad Muhammadans with clean-shaven heads and henna-dyed beards cut sugarcane into pieces, which lay in heaps before them, past the Hindu stall-keepers, who sold sweetmeats from round iron trays- balanced on little cane stools, till he came to the betel-leaf shop, where, surrounded by three large mirrors and lithographs of Hindu deities and beautiful European women, sat a dirty turbaned boy smearing the green, heartshaped betel leaves with red and white paint. A number of packets of 'Red-Lamp' and 'Scissors' cigarettes were arranged in boxes on his right and whole rows of biris native tobacco rolled in leaf on his left. From the reflection of his face in the looking-glass, which he shyly noticed, Bakha's eyes travelled to the cigarettes. He halted suddenly, and facing the shopkeeper with great humility, joined his hands and begged to know where he could put a coin to pay for a packet of 'Red-Lamp.' The shopkeeper pointed to a spot on the board near him. Bakha put his anna there. The betel-leaf-seller dashed some water over it from the jug with which he sprinkled the betel leaves now and again. Having thus purified it he picked up the nickel piece and threw it into the counter. Then he flung a packet of 'Red-Lamp' cigarettes at Bakha, as a butcher might throw a bone to an insistent dog sniffing round the corner of his shop.

Bakha picked up the packet and moved away. Then he opened it and took out a cigarette. He recalled that he had forgotten to buy a box of matches. He was too modest to go back, as though some deep instinct told him that as a sweeper-lad he should show himself in people's presences as little as possible. For a sweeper, a menial, to be seen smoking constituted an offence before the Lord. Bakha knew that it was considered a presumption on the part of the poor to smoke like the rich people. But he wanted to smoke all the same. Only he felt he should do so unobserved while he carried his broom and basket. He caught sight of a Muhammadan who was puffing at a big hubble-bubble sitting on a mattress spread on the dust at one of the many open-air barbers' stalls that gaudily flanked the way.

'Mian ji, will you oblige me with a piece of coal from your clay fire-pot?' he appealed.

'Bend down to it and light your cigarette, if that is what you want to do with the piece of coal,' replied the barber.

Bakha, not used to taking such liberties with anybody, even with the Muhammadans whom the Hindus considered outcastes and who were, therefore, much nearer him, felt somewhat embarrassed, but he bent down and lit his cigarette. He felt a happy, carefree man as he sauntered along, drawing the smoke and breathing it out through his nostrils. The coils of smoke rose slowly before his eyes and dissolved, but he was intent on the little white roll of tobacco which was becoming smaller every moment as its dark grey and red outer end smouldered away.

Passing through the huge brick-built gate of the town into the main street, he was engulfed in a sea of colour. Nearly a month had passed since he was last in the city, so little leisure did his job at the latrines allow him, and he couldn't help being swept away by the sensations that crowded in on him from every side. He followed the curves of the winding, irregular streets lined on each side with shops, covered with canvas or jute awnings and topped by projecting domed balconies. He became deeply engrossed in the things that were displayed for sale, and in the various people who thronged around them. His first sensation of the bazaar was of its smell, a pleasant aroma oozing from so many unpleasant things, drains, grains, fresh and decaying vegetables, spices, men and women and asafoetida. Then it was the kaleidoscope of colours, the red, the orange, the purple of the fruit in the tiers of baskets which were arranged around the Peshawari fruit-seller, dressed in a blue silk turban, a scarlet velvet waistcoat, embroidered with gold, a long white tunic and trousers; the gory red of the mutton hanging beside the butcher who was himself busy mincing meat on a log of wood, while his assistants roasted it on skewers over a charcoal fire, or fried it in the black iron pan; the pale-blond colour of the wheat shop; and the rainbow hues of the sweetmeat stall, not to speak of the various shades of turbans and skirts, from the deep black of the widows to the green, the pink, the mauve and the fawn of the newly-wedded brides, and all the tints of the shifting, changing crowd, from the Brahmin's white to the grass-cutter's coffee and the Pathan's swarthy brown.

Bakha felt confused, lost for a while. Then he looked steadily from the multi-coloured, jostling crowd to the beautifully arranged shops. There was the inquisitiveness of the child in his stare, absorbed here in the skill of a woodcutter and there in the manipulation of a sewing-machine by a tailor. 'Wonderful! Wonderful!' his instinct seemed to say, in response to the sights familiar to him and yet new. He caught the eye of Ganesh Nath, the bania, a sharp-tongued, mean little man, in view of whose pyramids of baskets full of flour, native sugar, dried chillies, peas and wheat he had sat begging for the gift of a tiny piece of salt and a smear of clarified butter. He withdrew his gaze immediately, because there had recently been a quarrel between the bania and his father on account of the compound interest Ganesh had demanded for the money Lakha had borrowed on the mortgage of his wife's trinkets to pay for her funeral. That was an unpleasant thing! He resisted the memory and drifted in his unconscious happiness towards the cloth shop where a big-bellied Lalla (Hindu gentleman), clad in an immaculately white loose muslin shirt, and loin-cloth was busy writing in curious hieroglyphics on a scroll book bound in ochre-coloured canvas, while his assistants unrolled bundles of Manchester cloth one after another, for inspection by an old couple from a village, talking incessantly the while of the 'tintint' and 'matchint,' just to impress the rustics into buying. Bakha was attracted by the woollen cloths that flanked the corners of the shop. That was the kind of cloth of which the sahibs' suits were made; the other cloth that he had seen lying before the yokels he could imagine turning soon into tunics and tehmets. All that was beneath his notice. But the woollen cloth, so glossy and nice! so expensive-looking! Not that he had any intention of buying, or any hope of wearing a kot-patloon suit; he felt for the money in his pocket to see if he had enough to pay an instalment on the purchase of cloth. There were only eight annas there. He remembered that he had promised to pay the babu's son for the English lesson. He crossed the street to where the Bengali sweetmeat-seller's shop was. His mouth began to water for the burfi, the sugar candy that lay covered with silver paper on a tray near the dirtily-clad, fat confectioner. 'Eight annas in my pocket,' he said to himself, 'dare I buy some sweets? If my father comes to know that I spend all my money on sweets,' he thought and hesitated, 'but come, I have only one life to live,' he said to himself, 'let me taste of the sweets; who knows, tomorrow I may be no more.' Standing in a corner, he stole a glance at the shop to see which was the cheapest thing he could buy. His eyes scanned the array of good things; rasgulas, gulabjamans and ludus. They were all so lushly, expensively smothered in syrup, that he knew they certainly could not be cheap, certainly not for him, because the shopkeepers always deceived the sweepers and the poor people, charging them much bigger prices, as if to compensate themselves for the pollution they courted by dealing with the outcastes. He caught sight of jalebis. He knew they were cheap. He had bought them before. He knew the rate at which they were sold, a rupee a seer (two pounds).

'Four annas' worth of jalebis,' Bakha said in a low voice as he courageously advanced from the corner where he had stood. His head was bent. He was vaguely ashamed and self-conscious at being seen buying sweets.

The confectioner smiled faintly at the crudeness of the sweeper's taste, for jalebis are rather coarse stuff and no one save a greedy low-caste man would ever buy four annas' worth of jalebis. But he was a shopkeeper. He affected a casual manner and picking up his scales abruptly, began to put the sweets in one pan against bits of stone and some black, round iron weights which he threw into the other. The alacrity with which he lifted the little string attached to the middle of the rod, balanced the scales for the shortest possible space of time and threw the sweets into a piece torn off an old *Daily Mail*, was as amazing as it was baffling to poor Bakha, who knew he had been cheated, but dared not complain. He caught the jalebis which the confectioner threw at him like a cricket ball, placed four nickel coins on the shoe-board for the confectioner's assistant who stood ready to splash some water on them, and he walked away embarrassed, yet happy.

His mouth was watering. He unfolded the paper in which the jalebis were wrapped and put a piece hastily into his mouth. The taste of the warm and sweet syrup was satisfying and delightful. He attacked the packet again. It was nice to fill one's mouth, he felt, because only then could you feel the full savour of the thing. It was wonderful to walk along like that, munching and looking at all the sights. The big signboards advertising the names of Indian merchants, lawyers and medical men, their degrees and professions, all in broad, huge blocks of letters, stared down at him from the upper stories of the shops. He wished he could read all the luridly painted boards. But he found consolation in recalling the arrangement he had made for beginning his lessons in English that afternoon. Then his gaze was drawn to a figure sitting in a window. He stared at her absorbed and un-self-conscious.

'Keep to the side of the road, you, low-caste vermin!' he suddenly heard someone shouting at him. 'Why don't you call, you swine, and announce your approach! Do you know you have touched me and defiled me, you cockeyed son of a bow-legged scorpion! Now I will have to go and take a bath to purify myself. And it was a new dhoti and shirt I put on this morning!'

Bakha stood amazed, embarrassed. He was deaf and dumb. His senses were paralysed. Only fear gripped his soul, fear and humility and servility. He was used to being spoken to roughly. But he had seldom been taken so unawares. The curious smile of humility which always hovered on his lips in the presence of high-caste men now became more pronounced. He lifted his face to the man opposite him, though his eyes were bent down. Then he stole a hurried glance at the man. The fellow's eyes were flaming and red-hot.

'You swine, you dog, why didn't you shout and warn me of your approach!' he shouted as he met Bakha's eyes. 'Don't you know, you brute, that you must not touch me!'

Bakha's mouth was open. But he couldn't utter a single word. He was about to apologise. He had already joined his hands instinctively. Now he bent his forehead over them, and he mumbled something. But the man didn't care what he said. Bakha was too confused in the tense atmosphere which surrounded him to repeat what he had said, or to speak coherently and audibly. The man was not satisfied with dumb humility.

'Dirty dog! Son of a bitch! The offspring of a pig!' he

shouted, his temper spluttering on his tongue and obstructing his speech, and the sense behind it, in its mad rush outwards. 'I . . . I'll have to go-o-o . . . and get washed—d—d . . . I . . . I was going to business and now . . . now, on account of *you*, I'll be late.'

A man had stopped alongside to see what was up, a white-clad man, wearing the distinctive dress of a rich Hindu merchant. The aggrieved one put his case before him, trying to suppress his rage all the while with his closed, trembling lips which hissed like a snake's:

'This dirty dog bumped right into me! So unmindfully do these sons of bitches walk in the streets! He was walking along without the slightest effort at announcing his approach, the swine!'

Bakha stood still, with his hands joined, though he dared to lift his forehead, perspiring and knotted with its hopeless and futile expression of meekness.

A few other men gathered round to see what the row was about, and as there are seldom any policemen about in Indian streets, the constabulary being highly corrupt, as it is drawn from amongst rogues and scoundrels, on the principle of 'set a thief to catch a thief,' the pedestrians formed a circle round Bakha, keeping at a distance of several yards from him, but joining in to aid and encourage the aggrieved man in his denunciations. The poor lad, confused still more by the conspicuous place he occupied in the middle of the crowd, felt like collapsing. His first impulse was to run, just to shoot across the throng, away, away, far away from the torment. But then he realised that he was surrounded by a barrier, not a physical barrier, because one push from his hefty shoulders would have been enough to unbalance the skeleton-like bodies of the Hindu merchants, but a moral one. He knew that contact with him, if he pushed through, would defile a great many more of these men. And he could already hear in his ears the abuse that he would thus draw on himself.

'Don't know what the world is coming to! These swine are

39

getting more and more uppish!' said a little old man. 'One of his brethren who cleans the lavatory of my house, announced the other day that he wanted two rupees a month instead of one rupee, and the food that he gets from us daily.'

'He walked like a Lat Sahib, like a Laften Gornor!' shouted the defiled one. 'Just think, folks, think of the enormity!'

'Yes, yes, I know,' chimed in a seedy old fellow, 'I don't know what the *kalijugs* of this age is coming to!'

'As if he owned the whole street!' exclaimed the touched man. 'The son of a dog!'

A street urchin, several of whom had pushed their way through people's legs to see the fun, took his cue from the vigorous complainant and shouted: 'Ohe, you son of a dog! Now tell us how you feel. You who used to beat us!'

'Now look, look,' urged the touched man, 'he has been beating innocent little children. He is a confirmed rogue!'

Bakha had stood mute so far. At this awkward concoction of the child's, his honest soul surged up in self-defence.

'When did I beat you?' he angrily asked the child.

'Now, now mark his insolence!' shouted the touched man. 'He adds insult to injury. He lies! look!'

'No, Lalla ji, it is not true that I beat this child, it is not true,' Bakha pleaded. 'I have erred now. I forgot to call. I beg your forgiveness. It won't happen again. I forgot. I beg your forgiveness. It won't happen again!'

But the crowd which pressed round him, staring, pulling grimaces, jeering and leering, was without a shadow of pity for his remorse. It stood unmoved, without heeding his apologies, and taking a sort of sadistic delight in watching him cower under the abuses and curses of its spokesman. Those who were silent seemed to sense in the indignation of the more vociferous members of the crowd, an expression of their own awakening lust for power.

To Bakha, every second seemed an endless age of woe and suffering. His whole demeanour was concentrated in humility, and in his heart there was a queer stirring. His legs trembled and shook under him. He felt they would fail him. He was really sorry and tried hard to convey his repentance to his tormentors. But the barrier of space that the crowd had placed between themselves and him seemed to prevent his feeling from getting across. And he stood still while they raged and fumed and sneered in fury; 'Careless, irresponsible swine!' 'They don't want to work.' 'They laze about!' 'They ought to be wiped off the surface of the earth!'

Luckily for Bakha, a tonga-wallah came up, goading a rickety old mare which struggled in its shafts to carry a jolting, bolting box-like structure and shouted a warning (for lack of a bell or a horn) for the crowd to disperse as he reined in his horse in time to prevent an accident. The crowd scattered to safety, blurting out vain abuse, exclamations of amusement and disgust, according to age and taste. The touched man was apparently not yet satisfied. He stood where he was, though aware that he would be forced to move by the oncoming vehicle, as for the first time for many years he had had an occasion to display his strength. He felt his four-foot-ten frame assume the towering stature of a giant with the false sense of power that the exertion of his will, unopposed against the docile sweeper-boy, had called forth.

'Look out, eh, Lalla ji,' shouted the tonga-wallah with an impudence characteristic of his profession. The touched man gave him an indignant, impatient look and signed to him, with a flourish of his hand, to wait.

'Don't you thrust your eyeballs at me,' the tonga-wallah answered back, and was going to move on, when, all of a sudden, he gripped his reins fast.

'You've touched me,' he had heard the Lalla say to Bakha. 'I will have to bathe now and purify myself anyhow. Well, take this for your damned irresponsibility, you son of a swine!' And the tonga-wallah heard a sharp, clear slap through the air.

Bakha's turban fell off and the jalebis in the paper bag in his hand were scattered in the dust. He stood aghast. Then his whole countenance lit with fire and his hands were no more joined. Tears welled up in his eyes and rolled down his cheeks. The strength, the power of his giant body glistened with the desire for revenge in his eyes, while horror, rage, indignation swept over his frame. In a moment he had lost all his humility, and he would have lost his temper too, but the man who had struck him the blow had slipped beyond reach into the street.

'Leave him, never mind, let him go, come along, tie your turban,' consoled the tonga-wallah, who being a Muhammadan and thus also an Untouchable from the orthodox Hindu point of view, shared the outcaste's resentment to a certain degree.

Bakha hurried aside and putting his basket and broom down, wrapped the folds of his turban anyhow. Then wiping the tears off his face with his hands he picked up his tools and started walking.

'You be sure to shout now, you illegally begotten!' said a shopkeeper from a side, 'if you have learnt your lesson!' Bakha hurried away. He felt that everyone was looking at him. He bore the shopkeeper's abuse silently and went on. A little later he slowed down, and quite automatically he began to shout: '*Posh* keep away, *posh*, sweeper coming, *posh*, *posh*, sweeper coming, *posh*, *posh*, sweeper coming!'

But there was a smouldering rage in his soul. His feelings would rise like spurts of smoke from a half-smothered fire, in fitful, unbalanced jerks when the recollection of some abuse or rebuke he had suffered kindled a spark in the ashes of remorse inside him. And in the smoky atmosphere of his mind arose dim ghosts of forms peopling the scene he had been through. The picture of the touched man stood in the forefront, among several indistinct faces, his bloodshot eyes, his little body with the sunken cheeks, his dry, thin lips, his ridiculously agitated manner, his abuse; and there was the circle of the crowd, jeering, scoffing, abusing, while he himself stood with joined hands in the centre. 'Why was all this?' he asked himself in the soundless speech of cells receiving and transmitting emotions, which was his usual way of communicating with himself. 'Why was all this fuss? Why was I so humble? I could have struck him! And to think that I was so eager to come to the town this morning. Why didn't I shout to warn the people of my approach? That comes of not looking after one's work. I should have begun to sweep the thoroughfare. I should have seen the high-caste people in the street. That man! That he should have hit me! My poor jalebis! I should have eaten them. But why couldn't I say something? Couldn't I have joined my hands to him and then gone away? The slap on my face! The coward! How he ran away, like a dog with his tail between his legs. That child! The liar! Let me come across him one day. He knew I was being abused. Not one of them spoke for me. The cruel crowd! All of them abused, abused, abused. Why are we always abused? The santry inspictor and the Sahib that day abused my father. They always abuse us. Because we are sweepers. Because we touch dung. They hate dung. I hate it too. That's why I came here. I was tired of working on the latrines every day. That's why they don't touch us, the high-castes. The tonga-wallah was kind. He made me weep telling me, in that way, to take my things and walk along. But he is a Muhammadan. They don't mind touching us, the Muhammadans and the sahibs. It is only the Hindus, and the out-castes who are not sweepers. For them I am a sweeper, sweeper—untouchable! Untouchable! Untouchable! That's the word! Untouchable! I am an Untouchable!'

Like a ray of light shooting through the darkness, the recognition of his position, the significance of his lot dawned upon him. It illuminated the inner chambers of his mind. Everything that had happened to him traced its course up to this light and got the answer. The contempt of those who came to the latrines daily and complained that there weren't any latrines clean, the sneers of the people in the outcastes' colony, the abuse of the crowd which had gathered round him this morning. It was all explicable now. A shock of which this was the name had passed through his perceptions, previously numb and torpid, and had sent a quiver into his being, stirred his nerves of sight, hearing, smell, touch and taste, all into a quickening. 'I am an Untouchable!' he said to himself, 'an Untouchable!' He repeated the words in his mind, for it was still a bit hazy and he felt afraid it might be immersed in the darkness again. Then, aware of his position, he began to shout aloud the warning word with which he used to announce his approach: '*Posh, posh*, sweeper coming.' The undertone, 'Untouchable, Untouchable,' was in his heart; the warning shout, '*Posh, posh*, sweeper coming!' was in his mouth. His pace quickened and it formed itself into a regular army stop into which his ammunition boots always fell so easily. He noticed that the thumping of his heavy feet on the ground excited too much attention. So he slowed down a little.

He became conscious that people were looking at him. He looked about himself to see why he was arousing all that attention. He felt the folds of his turban coming loose over his forehead. He wanted to retreat to a corner and tie it up properly. But he couldn't stop right in the middle, of the street. So he walked to a corner. Feeling that he might be observed, he assumed a look of abstraction, as if he was harassed by the thought of some important work he had in hand. And he stared round. He felt a fool knowing that he was acting. He unrolled his turban and began to wrap it hard round his head.

A bright, busy scene surrounded him where he lingered. The burning inside had emptied his mind of its content and he stood firm, struggling to express each shock as it impinged on his tight-stretched senses. A huge, big-humped, small-horned, spotted old brahminee bull was ruminating with half-closed eyes near him. The stink from its mouth as it belched, strangely unlike any odour which had assaulted Bakha's nostrils that day, was nauseating. And the liquid dung which the bull had excreted and which Bakha knew it was his duty to sweep off, sickened him. But presently he saw a well-dressed wrinkled old Hindu, wearing, like a rich man, a muslin scarf over his left shoulder, advance to the place where the bull was enjoying its siesta and touch the animal with his forefingers. That was a Hindu custom, Bakha knew. What the meaning of it was, he didn't know. His truant memory ran back to a scene which he had seen occur so many times in the town. The figure of a bull roaming aimlessly about, then walking leisurely up to a vegetable stall, sniffing at the row of baskets and getting away with a mouthful of cabbage, spinach or carrots. The keeper only abused it mildly, threatened it with his hand, without striking it. The bull moved a yard or two away munching the mouthful of vegetables it had purloined, and then it renewed its attack on the shop as soon as the keeper had turned his head away. 'How queer, the Hindus don't feed their cows although they call the cow "mother"!' Bakha thought. 'Their cattle which go to graze at the brookside are so skinny and feeble. Their cows can't yield more than two seers of milk a day.' He recalled with great self-righteousness, how when his father had a buffalo given him in charity (or rather out of superstition) by a rich Hindu merchant who desired sons and was advised by the Brahmins to bestow some cattle on the sweepers, they used to feed it daily with grain and tended it so well that it yielded twelve seers of milk a day. And these people feed their cows on mere remainders of food and even on the grain, sifted, as he well knew (for he had to do the sifting), from the cowdung. 'But they are kind to the cows. This bull must enjoy making its daily haul on those onions. That is why it smells.'

So far he had succeeded in isolating himself from his surroundings, but a cart came loaded with turnips and carrots and was emptied on to the ground. He stepped forward a few yards hurriedly. But a heap of decaying, rotten vegetables were littered over the baskets here. The putrid stink of this decomposing waste made him hurry away. He stared blankly for a while as he went along, without stirring his eyelids. The hot and crowded bazaar blazed with light. He was perspiring. His broad, frank face ordinarily so human, so variable, so changing, with its glistening high cheek-bones, its broad nose, the nostrils of which dilated

45

like those of an Arab horse, his fine full quivering underlip so alive always, was set and impassive, silent, a bit grim and deathly.

'*Posh, posh*, sweeper coming,' he whispered as he resumed his steps and advanced into what was neither a broad, busy street nor a narrow alley, but something of both, with a few odd shops occupied by companies of native bandsmen who play European instruments of music under the leadership of some retired army bandmaster, and are greatly in demand at the marriage and birth parties held in the gulleys of crowded cities. A stray grocer's shop or the betel-leaf-seller's punctuated the 'four-faced street' as it was called, and there was a modern flour mill to which went those fastidious old Indian women who loved coarse flour and could not digest the fine which was sold in the shops, or who loved economy and bought wheat wholesale and had it ground. An ancient oil-mill stood in a corner, in a large, dark room, in which the bullock went round and round revolving a wooden pestle into a wooden mortar fixed in the centre from the ceiling. Bakha had known this street ever since his childhood, was used to the deep pits and admired its straight barrack-like look. The English musical instruments and the gold-embroidered uniforms that hung from the band shops, especially in the shop of Jehangir, the celebrated owner of the finest band in the city, were very congenial to his English-apeing mind. He felt sobered by the comparative quiet of this street. The few shops in it made no claims on his attention and he felt less confused in its atmosphere. The sight of the brass instruments and uniforms in the band shop took his mind back to the military band of the 38th Dogras which he saw almost every day practising in the cantonment, and he partly forgot the insult and the injury which he had suffered; he felt soothed; his grief was assuaged.

Out of the silent street, he turned the corner under a house which bridged the thoroughfare and he went along a row of stalls where cheap nickel jewellery was being electroplated. As a child, Bakha had often expressed a desire to wear rings on his fingers, and liked to look at his mother adorned with silver ornaments. Now that he had been to the British barracks and known that the English didn't like jewellery, he was full of disgust for the florid, minutely studded designs of the native ornaments. So he walked along without noticing the big ear-rings and nose-rings and hair-flowers and other gold-plated ornaments which shone out from the background of green paper against which the smiths had ingeniously set them. A seller of cloth remnants loaded on a three-wheeled box-like carriage was haggling with some white-aproned Hindu women right in the middle of the street. Bakha waited for a minute to see if they would clear the road to enable him to pass. He was too tired to shout and stood awhile contemplating the cheap German lithographs of Hindu deities which a Sikh craftsman was fixing into expensive-looking frames. The picture of an Englishwoman, very scantily dressed and reclining with a flower in her hand, seduced Bakha's eyes away from the Hindu deities. The shopkeeper, noticing the basket and broom in Bakha's hand, gave him a stern look of disapproval and asked him to move on. The sweeper-boy lifted his face and pushing ahead called 'Posh, posh, sweeper coming' to the throng of buyers at the remnant-seller's stall. Dragging at the pieces of cloth and loudly bargaining, it was with difficulty that the irritable Mohammedan keeper of the stall could wrest his wares from the grasp of his customers or apprise them of the coming of the Untouchable. When, at last, he managed to do so, they dispersed, talking, whispering, furious, happy, melancholy, ahead of Bakha, and thronged round the bangle-sellers, who were shaking their glass wares to dazzle and attract the young brides in the crowd, who timidly walked behind their mothers and mothers-in-law, adorned in their gold-embroidered silk aprons and Benarsi skirts towards the temple where Bakha was going. He shouted his call again, a little wearily, 'Posh, posh, sweeper coming.' But the eager ardent women had forgotten the instigation of their last move and talking vociferously from their heaving, opera-star chests, did not listen till he reiterated his shout more vigorously.

At length he was allowed right of way and sighted the temple, a colossal, huge turreted structure of massive stone and carved masonry, the florid_exuberance of whose detailed and intricate decoration struck a strange kind of awe into his being. Bakha had never quite got over his sense of fear born of the respect for these twelve-headed and ten-armed gods and goddesses which was inculcated in him in his childhood. And as he looked up from the shadow of the high wall falling on the courtyard through which he was walking, he was impressed by some unknown force that seemed to lurk there and to make the place too heavy to breathe in. A few slate-coloured pigeons flew and rested in the little empty niches among the profuse carvings. The sight of them, so cool in their fawn-blue, and the sound of their cooing seemed to calm him. He surveyed the courtyard with the pertinacity of his sweeper's instinct, surveyed the droppings and the flowers, the heap of leaves and dust which he had come to clear.

He threw the basket and the broom he had in his hand on the ground and girt up his loins to attack his job as he, stood in the shadow of a banyan-tree that spread its dense foliage over the temple courtyard. A brass cage of a miniature temple with the beautifully polished image of a snake enclosed in it, lay on a small stone structure which surrounded the giant trunk of the banyan-tree. It arrested his attention. 'What is that snake image?' he asked himself casually. 'What does it mean? Perhaps a snake lives at the root of the tree,' his naïve mind answered. And he was slightly afraid, stepping away from the place instinctively. Then as he saw a regular stream of people pass through the courtyard after touching the foot of the altar of the miniature temple under the banyan-tree, his nerves were steadied. He drew near to the place where he had dropped his basket and his broom, shouting his call the while, lest the disaster of the morning be repeated through his negligence. This crowd was much more orthodox, this crowd which passed up and down the big broad stairs, in and out of the open doorway, this dense crowd, jostling in its blue, white, red and green trappings of cotton and silk. Bakha stared beyond the throng with his inner eye, not daring to look beyond the gate with the overt, lifted eye of the ordinary man curious to know, to solve a mystery, but like the slave stealing an enquiry into the affairs of his master. 'What have these people come here to worship?' he asked himself.

'*Ram*, Ram, *Sri*, *Sri*, *Hari*, *Narayan*, *Sri Krishna*,'[1] a devotee sang as he almost brushed past the Untouchable. '*Hey Hanuman jodah*,[2] *Kali Mai*.'[3]

Bakha had got his answer. The word 'Ram' he had heard very often, also 'Sri, Sri,' and he had seen a red shrine with a monkey carved on a wall, caged from without with brass bars—that he knew was called the shrine of Hanuman. The black shrine showing a jet-black woman with a flaming-red tongue, ten-armed and with a garland of skulls round her neck—that was called the shrine of Kali. Krishna was the blue god who played the flute in the coloured pictures of the betel-leaf-seller's shop in the street. But who was Hari, Narayan? And he was more completely baffled when a man passed by repeating: '*Om*, *Om*, *Shanti Deva*.'[4] Who was Shanti Deva? Was he in the temple?

'There is no chance of seeing anything if I stand here,' he mused. 'I shall go and look.' But he hadn't the courage to go. He felt weak. He realised that an Untouchable going into a temple polluted it past purification. His father would be angry if he knew that he hadn't done any work this morning. Somebody might come and see him roaming about and think he was a thief.

But the edge of his curiosity became more and more acute as he stood there. He suddenly dismissed his thoughts and with

---

[1] Names of various incarnations of the supreme god.

[2] The monkey god who helped Rama, the hero of the Ramayana, to fight against his enemy Ravana.

[3] The supreme god in its female form as the divine mother.

[4] An invocation to the gods.

a determined, hurried step went towards the stairs, looking to this side and that, with a tense, heavy head, but unafraid. A murderer might have advanced 'like that, one confident in his consummate mastery of the art of killing. But he soon lost his grace in the low stoop which the dead weight of years of habitual bending cast on him. He became the humble, oppressed under-dog that he was by birth, afraid of everything, creeping slowly up,, in a curiously hesitant, cringing movement. After he had mounted the first two steps, he stood completely demoralised with fear and retreated to the place from which he had started. He picked up his broom by its short wooden handle and began to sweep the ground. The particles of dust flew in a small, very small cloud before him, pale white and radiating bright gleams of gold where the sun-rays touched them. But Bakha didn't notice that. To him the litter of banyan leaves, flower petals, the droppings of pigeons, stray sticks and the dust, which his broom soon collected in its sweep, was more immediate, though even of this he was fairly unmindful till the dust flew to his nostrils and he tied the edge of his turban across his nose. And he jogged along, slowly and slowly, step by step, with an apathy peculiar to him. This was a slow business as compared to the work at the latrines, but though slow and wearying, not so unpleasant.

He collected the litter in small heaps, because he knew he could not push any more of it with his small broom, right round the courtyard. He had purposed to collect these small heaps, one by one, in his basket later on. When the heaps were ready, he waited for a moment to wipe the sweat off his brow. The temple stood challengingly before him. He bent down and began to collect the heaps which his broom had piled up. The unfailing sense of direction of his inner impulse landed him near the steps of the temple again. But now he was afraid. The temple seemed to advance towards him like a monster, and to envelop him. He hesitated for a while. Then his will strengthened. With a sudden onslaught he had captured five steps of the fifteen that led to the door of the temple. There he stopped, his heart drumming fiercely in his chest, which bent forward like that of an athletic runner on the starting-line, his head thrown back. The force of another impulse pushed him a step or two further up. Here he was almost thrown out of equilibrium by an accidental knock on his knee and stood tottering, threatened with a fall. But he gripped the steps hard, and recovering his balance, rushed headlong to the top step. From here, as he lay, he could peer through with his head raised above the marble threshold, lowered (luckily for him) by the rubbings of the heads of the devout, and affording a glimpse, just a glimpse, of the sanctuary which had so far been a secret, a hidden mystery to him. In the innermost recesses of the tall, dark sanctum, beyond the brass gates, past what seemed. a maze of corridors, Bakha's eyes probed the depths of a raised platform. There, from a background of gold-embroidered silk and velvet draperies, stood out various brass images dimly shrouded in the soft tremors of incense that rose from a dish at their feet. A priest sat half naked, with a tuft of hair on the top of his shaven head, unduly prominent as it tied itself in an inscrutable knot. An open book lay on a bookstand before him, amidst the paraphernalia of brass utensils, conch-shells and other ritualistic objects. A tall man, evidently also a priest, naked, save for a loin-cloth, darkhaired and supple, with a sacred thread throwing into relief the beautiful curves of his graceful body, got up and blew a conch-shell. Bakha saw, peered, stared hard, and realised that the morning service had begun. After the loud soprano of '*Om, Shanti Deva*'[1] the seated priest lifted his hard voice, jarring on the bell which tinkled in his left hand, into unison with the brass notes of the conch. The quiet little shrine of a moment ago had become a living, feeling reality. Worshippers flocked from the inner corridors of the temple towards the platform of the gods, and stood beneath the dome, singing '*Arti, Arti* . . .'[2] in a chorus. The loud flourish of the first

---

[1] An invocation to the gods.

[2] Idem.

conch note floated into a sweet, lingering melody, soft and clear, yet potent with a strength of the most mysteriously affecting kind, a strength sustained enough to raise one's hair, as it proceeded to a finish in the last hoarse shout of triumphant worship: '*Sri Ram Chandar ki Jai*' (Long live the Great God Ram).

Bakha was profoundly moved. He was affected by the rhythm of the song. His blood had coursed along the balanced melodic line to the final note of strength with such sheer vigour that his hands joined unconsciously, and his head hung in the worship of the unknown god.

But a cry disturbed him: 'Polluted, polluted, polluted.' A shout rang through the air. He was completely unnerved. His eyes were covered with darkness. He couldn't see anything. His tongue and throat were parched. He wanted to utter a cry, a cry of fear, but his voice failed him. He opened his mouth wide to speak. It was no use. Beads of sweat covered his forehead. He tried to raise himself ftom the awkward attitude of prostration, but his limbs had no strength left in them. For a second he was as if dead.

Then as suddenly as he had been overpowered he asserted himself. He lifted his head and looked round. The scales fell from his eyes. He could see the little man with a drooping moustache whom he knew to be a priest of the temple, racing up the courtyard, trembling, stumbling, tottering, falling, with his arms lifted in the air, and in his mouth the hushed cry 'polluted, polluted, polluted.'

'I have been seen, undone,' the sentence quickly flashed across Bakha's mind. But he espied the figure of a woman behind the shouting priest. He stood amazed, though, still afraid, still feeling that he was doomed. He was unaware, however, of the form the doom would take.

But he soon knew. A thumping crowd of worshippers rushed out of the temple, and stood arrayed as in the grand finale of an opera show. The lanky little priest stood with upraised hands, a few steps below him. His sister, Sohini (for that was the woman he had seen behind the priest), lingered modestly in the courtyard.

'Polluted, polluted, polluted!' shouted the Brahmin below. The crowd above him took the cue and shouted after him, waving their hands, some in fear, others in anger, but all in a terrible orgy of excitement. One of the crowd struck out an individual note.

'Get off the steps, you scavenger! Off with you! You have defiled our whole service You have defiled our temple! Now we will have to pay for the purificatory ceremony. Get down, get away, you dog!'

Bakha ran down the steps, past the priest below him, to his sister. He had two impulses, that of fear for himself, for the crime he knew he had committed, another of fear for his sister, for the crime she might have committed, since she stood there speechless.

'You people have only been polluted from a distance,' Bakha heard the little priest shriek. 'I have been defiled by contact.'

The distance, the distance!' the worshippers from the top of the steps were shouting. 'A temple can be polluted according to the Holy Books by a low-caste man coming within sixty-nine yards of it, and here he was actually on the steps, at the door. We are ruined. We will need to have a sacrificial fire in order to purify ourselves and our shrine.'

'But I . . . I . . .' shouted the lanky priest histrionically, and never finished his sentence.

The crowd on the temple steps believed that he had suffered most terribly, and sympathised, for it had seen the sweeper-boy rush past him. They didn't ask about the way he had been polluted. They didn't know the story that Sohini told Bakha at the door of the courtyard with sobs and tears.

'That man, that man,' she said, 'that man made suggestions to me, when I was cleaning the lavatory of his house there. And when I screamed, he came out shouting that he had been defiled.'

Bakha rushed back to the middle of the courtyard, dragging his sister behind him, and he searched for the figure of the priest in the crowd. The man was no longer to be seen, and even the surging crowd seemed to show its heels as it saw the giant stride of the sweeper advance frighteningly towards the temple. Bakha stopped still in his determined advance when he saw the crowd fly back. His fist was clenched. His eyes flared wild and red, and his teeth ground between them the challenge: 'I could show you what that Brahmin dog has done!'

He felt he could kill them all. He looked ruthless, a deadly pale and livid with anger and rage. A similar incident he had heard about, rose to his mind in a flash. A young rustic had teased a friend's sister as she was coming home through the fields after collecting fuel. Her brother had gone straight to the fields with an axe in his hand and murdered the fellow. 'Such an insult!' he thought. 'That he should attack a young and innocent girl. And then the hypocrisy of it! This man, a Brahmin, he lies and accuses me of polluting him, after—father of fathers, I hope he didn't violate my sister.' A suspicion stole into his mind that he might have. He was stung to the quick, and turning to Sohini asked her loudly:

'Tell me, tell me, that he didn't do anything to you!'

Sohini was weeping. She shook her head in negation. She couldn't speak.

Bakha was reassured a bit. 'But no, the attempt!' he thought; 'the man must have made indecent suggestions to her. I wonder what he did. Father of fathers! I could kill that man. I could kill that man!' He was being tormented with the anxiety to know what had really happened, and yet he hesitated to question his sister again lest she should begin to cry. But his doubts and misgivings about her were too much for him.

'Tell me, Sohini,' he said, turning fiercely to his sister, how far did he go?'

She sobbed and didn't reply.

'Tell me! Tell me! I will kill him if . . .' he shouted.

'He-e-e just teased me,' she at last yielded. 'And then when I was bending down to work, he came and held me by my breasts.'

'The son of a pig!' Bakha exclaimed. 'I will go and kill him!'
And he rushed blindly towards the courtyard.

'No, no. Come back. Let's go away,' called Sohini after
him, arresting his progress by dragging hard at a lapel of his
overcoat.

He stood staring at the temple for a moment. There was not
a soul to be seen out of doors. All was still. He felt the cells of
his body lapse back chilled. His eyes caught sight of the
magnificent sculptures over the doors extending right up to the
pinnacle. They seemed vast and fearful and oppressive. He was
cowed back. The sense of fear came creeping into him. He felt
as if the gods were staring at him. They looked so real although
they were not like anything he had ever seen on earth. They
seemed hard, their eyes fixed as they ogled out of their niches,
with ten arms and five heads. He bent his head low. His eyes
were dimmed. His clenched fists relaxed and fell loosely by his
side. He felt weak and he wanted support. It was with difficulty
that he steadied his gait and retraced his steps, with Sohini, to the
outer gate.

The sight of her walking along with him, however, sent a
wave of anguish into his soul. So frail she, looked and so
beautiful. Bakha was conscious of the charm of his sister. Her
slim, pale-brown figure, soft and warm and glowing, shot
through with a lustre that set off her ornaments, the rings in her
ears, the bangles on her arms, to a ravishing effect, was so silent
and subtly modest and full of a strange tenderness and light. He
could not think of her brutalised by anyone, even by a husband
married to her according to the rites of religion. He looked at her
and somehow a picture of her future life seemed to come before
him. She had a husband—a man who had her, possessed her. He
loathed the ghost of her would-be husband that he conjured up.
He could see the stranger holding her full breasts and she
responding with a modest acquiescence. He hated the thought of
that man touching her. He felt he would be losing something. He
dared not think what he would be losing. He dared not think that

he himself—'I am her brother,' he said to himself, to rectify his thoughts which seemed to be going wrong. But there seemed no difference to his naked mind between his own feeling for her and what might be a husband's love. He dismissed the whole picture. Facing his mind was the figure of the little priest. That made his blood boil. He felt a wild desire to retaliate, retaliation meaning to him just doing anything to the man, from belabouring him with blows to killing him if need be. For though the serfdom of thousands of years had humbled him, the tropical emotions that welled up in him under an open sky had lessened his respect for life. He came of peasant stock, his ancestors having come down in the social scale by their change of profession. The blood of his peasant ancestors, free to live their own life even though they may have been slaves, raced in him now.

'I could have given him a bit of my mind,' he exclaimed to himself.

A superb specimen of humanity he seemed whenever he made the high resolve to say something, to go and do something, his fine form rising like a tiger at bay. And yet there was a futility written on his face. He could not overstep the barriers which the conventions of his superiors had built up to protect their weakness against him. He could not invade the magic circle which protects a priest from attack by anybody, especially by a low-caste man. So in the highest moment of his strength, the slave in him asserted itself, and he lapsed back, wild with torture, biting his lips, ruminating his grievances.

A busy street lay before the brother and sister when they emerged from the temple. Bakha looked out to it vaguely. He could not concentrate on the riot of variety that was displayed in it. He had no patience to see anything or to hear anything, and he didn't want to speak. 'Why didn't I go and kill that hypocrite!' he cried out silently. 'I could have sacrificed myself for Sohini. Everyone will know about her. My poor sister! How can she show her face to the world after this? But why didn't she let me go and kill that man? Why was she born a girl in our house to bring disgrace upon us? So beautiful! So beautiful and so accursed! I wish she had been the ugliest woman in the world! Then no one would have teased her!' But he couldn't bear the thought of her being ugly. His pride in her beauty seemed to be hurt. And he just wished: 'Oh, God, why was she born, why was she born.' Then, however, he saw her bending and wiping her eyes with her apron. With a sudden burst of tenderness and humility he gripped her arm close and dragged her along, writhing with the conflicts in his soul, trembling with despair.

A few steps and he felt more easy. His breath came and went more evenly. His big, raw-boned body, strung into a lithe, active frame by his overpowering passion, became rather heavy. His instinctive fear of the people in the street, all so quick to notice the vagaries of individuals, rude and ill-mannered if they saw something ridiculous or sublime, made him recollect himself. He contemplated his experience now in the spirit of resignation which he had inherited through the long centuries down through his countless outcaste ancestors, fixed, yet flowing like a wave, confirmed at the beginning of each generation by the discipline of the caste ideal.

'Do you go home, Sohini,' he said to his sister, who walked behind him, ashamed and crestfallen, with the stain upon her honour she thought it was to have been the object of a scene. 'Yes, do you go home,' he said, 'and I'll go and get the food. Take this basket and broom with you.'

She moved her head in assent without looking up at him. Then she took the basket and broom from his hand and drawing her apron to cover her face, she walked away towards the city gates.

A glance in the direction of his sister, and Bakha walked slowly away from the house of God. '*Posh, posh,* sweeper coming,' he suddenly remembered his warning call, as he just avoided touching a barefooted shopkeeper who was running like a holy bull from shop to shop. When he had thus unconsciously passed through the congested iron-monger's bazaar, past a humanity whose panting rush in its varied, rather hybrid clothes, neither English nor Indian, he took for granted, he found himself standing outside an alley which spread like a yawn between a fruit shop and an old perfumer's. Beneath the emptiness in his inside lay suppressed a confusion arising from the overpowering contradictions of his feelings. But outwardly he was calm and unperturbed. He stood still for a moment, to exercise his sense of direction, as he had been walking almost in a coma. 'To the houses in this alley for food,' he said to himself and turned into the lane.

A stray dog, thin, flea-bitten and diseased, was relieving itself. Another which was all bones, was licking at some decayed food on a refuse-heap that lay blocking the drain. Right across the passage further up lay a cow. Bakha observed the dirt and filth that lay about, casually. But the animals seemed to infuriate him. He approached the dogs, and jumping sharply surprised them into making off with a squeak and a squeal. The bovine insensibility of the cow that lay stretched before him was, however, hard to break through. Lest he should be accused of disturbing the holy mother by the rich owners at whose doors she lay stretched, he held it by the horns to protect his legs against its well-known ferocity, and picked his way across. More heaps of rubbish littered all over the small, old brick pavement meant to him only more reminders of his sister's careless performance of her duties that morning. He excused her, however, by thinking of her suffering. Nobody who had been insulted as she had, could be expected to do her work properly. He didn't want to confess that his defence of her was unreasonable, in that she was supposed to have been here before she went to clean the house in the temple. A huge din of coppersmiths hammering and rehammering copper in their irregular little dark shops engulfed him and he walked more comfortably for a while, for the noise was pleasant, even cheering from a distance, and helped to drown his conscience with regard to his sister's negligence. Deeper in the square, however, the 'thak, thak, thak' that issued from the collection of shops became unbearable. He would have rushed into the little sub-alley where he had to go and call for food but that the ablutions of a devout Hindu on the platform of the street well in the middle of the lane offered the prospect of Bakha getting well sprinkled with the holy water that rained off from the well-oiled body, naked save for a loin-cloth. Bakha waited until his holiness had emptied a canful of water on his head and slung the empty vessel back into the well. Then he sauntered into the dark, damp gulley, where two fat men could hardly pass each other. He felt calmer because it was cool here and the noise of the copper-beaters was fainter. But the test of his nerves was yet to come. For being an outcaste he could not insult the sanctity of the houses by climbing the stairs to the top floors where the kitchens were, but had to shout and announce his arrival from below.

'Bread for the sweeper, mother. Bread for the sweeper,' he called, standing at the door of the first house. His voice died down to the echo of 'thak, thak, thak,' which stole into the alley.

'The sweeper has come for bread, mother! The sweeper has come for the bread,' he shouted a little louder.

But it was of no avail.

He penetrated further into the alley, and standing near a point where the doors of four houses were near each other, he shouted his call: 'Bread for the sweeper, mother; bread for the sweeper.'

Yet no one seemed to hear him on the tops of the houses. He wished it had been the afternoon, because he knew that at that time the housewives were always downstairs sitting in the halls of their houses, or on the drains in the gulley, gossiping or plying the spinning-wheel. But the vision of a number of them squatting in the gulley and wailing with each other's aprons over their heads, or beating their breasts in mourning for the dead, came before his eyes and he felt shy.

'Bread for the sweeper, mother,' he shouted again.

There was no response. His legs were aching. There was a

lethargy in his bones, a curious numbness. His mind refused to work. Feeling defeated, he sat down on the wooden platform of a house in the lane. He was tired and disgusted, more tired than disgusted, for he had almost forgotten the cause of his disgust, his experiences of the morning. A sort of sleepiness seemed to steal into his bones. He struggled hard against it by keeping his eyes open. Then he tightly leaned against the hard wood of the huge hall door as a concession to his fatigued limbs. He knew that his place was on the damp brick pavement on the side of the drain which carried water from the filth-pipes of all the houses. But for a while he simply didn't care. Bringing his legs together he crouched into a corner and gave himself up to the soft urgings of the darkness that seemed to envelop him. Before long he had succumbed to sleep.

Unfortunately for his tired body, it was ān uneasy half sleep that he enjoyed, the hindrances in the labyrinthine depths of his unconscious weaving strange, weird fantasies and dreams. He saw himself driven in a bullock-cart through the thronging streets of a most marvellous city, encountering a wedding procession of gaily-dressed, laughing people, preceded by a litter, covered with ochre-coloured draperies, carried by four men, who were themselves preceded by a Sikh band, dressed in the uniform of the English Army, carrying clarinets, bugles, flutes,.super-saxophones and drums, walking in loose formation, and playing not the harmonies which he had heard in the cantonment, but tuneless wails, weird and disturbing. Then he was on the platform of a railway station. Before him stood a train of forty closed iron freight wagons with an engine at each end. Somewhere in a long row he could espy open trucks, two laden with boulders of stone and bulks of timber. He saw himself getting onto the top of one of these loads and sitting there, a bundle by his side, an umbrella with a carved silver handle in his hand, a solar topee on his head and the tube of his father's hookah in his mouth. Suddenly he could see the closed iron freight wagons move. Almost simultaneously he could hear squeaks, creaks, execrations, lamentations and general excitement, as if someone had been murdered on a near but invisible siding. Full of fear and pity he imagined himself bending over the end of the wagon. He discovered that they were only some blue-uniformed railway coolies pushing a coach into a shed. He was next transplanted to a small village with very narrow streets, muddy and heavily cambered with rills of water running on either side. He could see cows wandering about and two big carts, heavy laden, get stuck in the slush as they came from opposite directions. A number of sparrows alighted on the heaps of grain in the open shops and helped themselves to food. A carrion crow soared down to the bruised neck of a bullock and began to peck at it. Then he watched a little girl who stood outside a sweet-shop. The child advanced smiling, holding aloft the food she had bought. The crow swooped down and snatched at her hand and threw her food onto the heap of litter lying near the gutter. She began to cry. A silversmith, handsome, immense, who had sat before a charcoal fire fashioning ornaments, looked up, smiled understandingly, and with his tongs placed a burning ember on her uplifted hand. The child toddled off happily through a narrow entry, pleased that she was carrying the nucleus of warmth for her mother's hearth . . . Then Bakha saw himself in the compound of a school where boys in yellow turbans were reading aloud as their master sat, cane in hand, exercising a vigilant scrutiny over his wards. The monitor of the class passed successively to each of his fellows on the benches a verse which they declaimed after him. Behind a network of streets in the wonder city ran a stream by which stood a palace, whose domed inner roof was supported by stone trusses and whose wealth of stone carving compelled attention. Bakha looked at it with wonder and admiration and gasped. He entered and saw how it had been hewed out of a rock. Its roof was painted in red and gold and black and green. By colonnades of immense and richly ornamented columns forming a nave and an aisle at the far end, stood men crowding round an emaciated man. Out of the dome some soldiers emerged and chattering, talking, smiling, happy, they carried him to a vast plain, a burning-ground, where the embers of the incinerations of the previous evening still smouldered, sending delicate spirals of smoke from the mounds of human bodies. A number of holy men stood beside the dead bodies, pouring the ashes of the dead into their hair, drinking hemp and dancing in an orgy of destruction. A gora sahib was looking on from a corner. He smiled at the scene. Bakha saw one of the holy men, an ascetic whose years were said to exceed ten thousand and who sat naked and with shaven head in silent contemplation, perform a magic trick by which the sahib was turned into a little black dog. Bakha thought of offering him a gift but the holy man's followers told him he shouldn't. Bakha stood wondering how the man lived. Then a swarm of monkeys jumped down from a tree and—

'*Alakh, alakh*'[1] came a call and awoke him. The dream completely faded out in the glare that the sunshine cast leaning over the tall houses. Bakha knew it was noon and that just at that time every holy man and beggar seeks the doors of the devout for alms which he has earned by the dedication of his person to God. Almost at once he collected himself together, rubbed his eyes and felt: 'I shall soon get bread.' He knew that the housewives sat waiting for the ash-smeared sadhus (ascetics) and did not eat their food before dispensing hospitality to the holy men. 'I shall soon get food,' he thought, and he looked up at the sadhu without getting up. The man was staring down at him. Bakha fell back into the drowsy listlessness of a moment ago.

'*Bham, bham, bhole Nath*,'[2] cried the sadhu in the peculiar lingo of Sadhuhood, shaking the bangles on his arms, which brought two women rushing to the terraces of their house-tops.

'I am bringing the food, sadhu ji,' shouted the lady at whose doorstep Bakha was at rest. But she stopped short when she saw the sweeper's body knotted up on the wooden platform outside her house.

---

[1] An invocation of the ascetics.

[2] Idem.

'You eater of your masters,' she shouted, 'may the vessel of your life never float in the sea of existence! May you perish and die! You have defiled my house! Go! Get up, get up! You eater of your masters! Why didn't you shout if you wanted food? Is this your father's house that you come and rest here?'

Bakha got up as abruptly as the woman's tone had changed from kindness to the holy man to cruelty to him. And rubbing his eyes and trying to shake off the lethargy that lay thick like hot air about him, he apologised.

'Forgive me, mother. I shouted for bread, but you were perhaps busy and didn't hear me. I was tired and sat down.'

'But, you eater of your masters! why did you sit down on my doorstep, if you had to sit down at all? You have defiled my religion! You should have sat there in the gulley! Now I will have to sprinkle holy water all over the house! You spoiler of my salt! Oh, how terrible! You sweepers have lifted your heads to the sky, nowadays! This bad luck on a Tuesday morning too! And after I had been to the temple! . . .' She saw the sadhu waiting and checked her copious flow of remonstrance and abuse. Bakha didn't look up to her but he knew she was dark with anger.

'Be patient, sadhu ji,' her voice came again. 'I shall just go and get you your food. This eater of his masters has even burnt the bread I was baking by detaining me here.' She retreated from her vantage point on the terrace.

Meanwhile the other woman, as quiet as she was heavy, came down the stairs with a handful of rice in one hand and a chapati in the other. The first she put into the holy man's bag, the second she handed over to Bakha, adding kindly: 'My child, you shouldn't sit on people's doorstops like this.'

'May you live long and all your family prosper!' said the sadhu as he received the alms. 'Isn't there a little lentil of which you could make the holy man a gift?'

'Yes, sadhu ji,' she said, 'to-morrow, from to-morrow, you shall have lentil! I am busy cooking.' And she rushed upstairs saying she was busy cooking.

The owner of the defiled house came down now, as voluble as she was short of volume. She stared eagle-eyed at Bakha and remonstrated: 'Wah! You have wrought strange work this morning, defiling my home!' Then she turned to the holy man and heaped a steaming hot vegetable curry and a potful of cooked rice onto the sadhu's black skull of a begging-bowl. 'Please accept this,' she said, 'the house is all right; he didn't really pollute it. I wonder if you have a cure for my son's fever which you could bring me.'

'May the gods bless you and your children,' said the holy man. 'I will bring you some herbs in the morning.' And he turned his back after having exacted his dues for looking after the souls of his disciples.

'May you die,' the woman cursed Bakha, thinking she had acquired enough merit by being good to the holy man and wouldn't lose much of it by being unkind to the sweeper. 'What have you done to earn your food to-day, you or your sister? She never cleaned the lane this morning, and you have defiled my home. Come, clean the drain a bit and then you can have this bread. Come, do a bit of work now that you have defiled my home.'

Bakha looked at the lady for a while. Then cowed down by her abuse, he set to work to sweep the gutter with a small broom which, he knew, his sister always hid under the wooden platform where he, sat.

'Mother,' shouted a little child from the top of the house, 'I want to go to the lavatory.'

'No, you can't go,' replied the mother, who stood superintending the sweeper's work. 'You can't go upstairs, it will lie there all day,' she said. 'Come here, come downstairs, quick, and go here in the drain. The sweeper will clear it away.'

'No,' insisted the obstinate boy, who felt shy to sit in a public place.

His mother rushed up to fetch him. She had forgotten to give Bakha the bread she had brought for him. On reaching the top of her house she sent her son without the bread, and since she didn't want to undertake another journey down. she called to Bakha while he was in the middle of his job.

'*Vay* Bakhya, take this. Here's your bread coming down.' And she flung it at him.

Bakha laid aside the broom and tried hard to be the good cricketer he usually was, but the thin, paper-like pancake floated in the air and fell like a kite on to the brick pavement of the gully. He picked it up quietly and wrapped it in a duster with the other bread he had received. He was too disgusted to clean the drain after this, especially as the little boy sat relieving himself before him. He threw the little broom aside and made off without saying a thank-you.

'Aren't they a superior lot these days!' exclaimed the lady, disappointed at not receiving a courtesy. 'They are getting more and more uppish.'

'I have finished, mother,' her son shouted.

'Rub yourself on the ground, my child, if there is no one to give you water at the pickle-maker's next door,' she said, and she went back to her kitchen.

All the accumulated fury of the morning was in Bakha's soul and the rage of this fresh insult. He felt that he had got up from his sleep almost cured of the unpleasant memories of the morning, but now there was an ache in the back of his head. A subtle heat was mounting from his spine, drying the blood in his body and shrinking his face. 'I wish that hadn't happened at the temple,' he said to himself. 'Then Sohini would have come for the bread. Why did I come to the lane?' He moved in a sort of trance. Black and filthy, yet orderly with that dignity and decorum which his exotic dress gave him, he was possessed by a curious fire. 'I shouldn't have picked up that bread from the pavement,' he said, and he sighed. That seemed to relax him.

Meanwhile he began to feel hungry as if rats were running about in his belly searching for food. He began to spit a white flocculent spittle on the dust as he hurried out of the town, homewards. His limbs sagged. He felt the sweat trickling down his face from under his turban as soon as he got into the open. He looked up to the sun. It stood right above him. Bakha's face quickened with the awareness of the sun 'coming on.' His body had a wonderful time sense, as it really had a sense of other things. 'How can I go home with only two chapatis under my arm?' the feeling came to him. 'Father will be sure to ask if I have brought any delicacies. It isn't my fault that I have only two cakes. He is sure to ask why Sohini didn't go down to get the food. I shall have to tell him the whole story. He will be angry!' He remembered how, when he was a child, his father had abused him because he came and reported that a sepoy had frightened him. 'Father always takes sides with the others. Never with his own family. How can I tell him about the priest? He won't believe it. And he will burst out if I say anything about the incident in the street: "The only day that I send you down to the town to work, you go and pick a quarrel." That is what he will say: "When will you learn to do your job properly?" ' Bakha felt that rather than bear this he would go and tell a lie. 'But then he is sure to know because Sohini didn't go to fetch the food. He must have asked her why she came home so early. Perhaps it will be best not to say anything. But he is sure to ask. Oh, never mind, let come what may.' And he closed his mind to the conflict, and became absorbed in a stray eagle and a few specks of cloud.

With a mind occupied by things, Bakha didn't find the way home very long. He could see his family basking in the sunshine outside the house. There was no provision for lights in the sweepers' street, so most of the inhabitants compensated themselves for the nights spent in utter darkness amid the smoke of smouldering hearth fires in their small congested houses, by spending most of their time in the open air. In the summer, of course, this was difficult, even though they made awnings of the string beds on which they slept at night, by covering them with coarse, unwanted rags of jute cloth, and sat under them all day.

During the winter, however, they came out of their homes as soon as the sun was up and lived out in it till the evening fell and it was too cold.

Sohini had kept up the outdoor kitchen which her mother had made adjoining the door of her house. It was not strictly a kitchen in the Hindu manner, for there were no four lines defining its limits, according to those laws of hygiene which are the basis of Hindu piety. A couple of brooms stood out next to the fireplace, an empty refuse-basket, a can, two earthen pitchers and a chipped enamelled jug lay scattered about. Most of the utensils were of clay, darkened by the soot of many fires, and never washed since Bakha's mother had died, for Sohini was young and inexperienced, and had a great deal too much work to do outside the house to devote herself assiduously to housework. Besides, there was a scarcity of water. And since, on account of their profession and the filthy surroundings in which they were forced to live, they needed more than a pitcherful of water, but could not get it, they just did without; till sanitation, cleanliness and hygiene had lost its meaning for them.

'Where is Rakha?' Bakha asked his sister, as he gave her the duster containing the bread.

She kept quiet, but Lakha, his father, answered:

'The rascal has gone to get food at the *langar* (the kitchen) in the barracks.'

The old man was sitting on his bedstead, now stretched out near the kitchen, puffing away at his hookah, each puff a short asthmatic cough. He looked well groomed. He had evidently been plucking superfluous hair from his face with a pair of tweezers which he always kept under his pillow near a painted native looking-glass, because his bristling white beard looked trimmed up into clean edges and sides. There was a kindly look in his eyes due probably to the easy and comfortable morning he had had. But his lips were tightly set and his brow was wrinkled under his cleanly tied blue turban. Grumpiness was not too far away from him to summon if need be.

'Have you brought anything nice to eat?' he asked Bakha. 'I am just hungering for some pickles, spinach and maize-flour bread.'

'I have brought only two chapatis,' replied Bakha. The feeling came to him which had possessed him throughout his journey, of the struggle between making a clean breast of it all and lying.

'You are a good-for-nothing scoundrel,' muttered Lakha. 'I hope that the rascal brings something nice from the barracks.'

As he said so the Jemadar's mouth watered and his mind travelled to the great big piles of cooked food which he had received on the occasion of marriages in the alleys of the city. There were fried bread and chingri puffs, vegetables, curries and semolina pudding, sweets and tasty pickles—remainders from the trays of high-caste men, and sometimes portions direct from the kitchens. Those were unforgettable days, so pleasing to Lakha that he had always watched the development of each and every girl in the alleys where he worked and asked their parents when the auspicious occasion of their marriage would be celebrated. It may be that Lakha is to blame for most of the child marriages in Bulashah. The parents of the potential brides always remembered Lakha, giving him a suit of clothes and generous portions of food. Another occasion he remembered was when the regiment, to which he was attached, came back from the war, for during the rejoicings on its return there were grand feasts, and he, as the Jemadar of all the sweepers, was in charge of the distribution of the remainders of food. He recalled how the wooden box where his wife kept sweets was never empty that year.

'I don't know the people in the town very well, and I didn't call at all the houses for food,' said Bakha to excuse himself to his father. The remark disturbed Lakha's gastronomic fantasy.

'You should try and get to know them. You have got to work for them all your life, my son, after I die.'

Bakha felt the keen edge of his sense of anticipation draw before his eyes the horrible prospect of all the future days of service in the town and the insults that would come with them. He could see himself being shouted at by a crowd; he could see a little priest fling his arms in the air and cry, 'defiled, defiled.' He could see the lady who had thrown the bread down at him reprimanding him for not cleaning the gutter. 'No, no,' his mind seemed to say, 'never,' and there appeared before him the vague form of a Bakha clad in a superior military uniform, cleaning the commodes of the sahibs in the British barracks. 'Yes, much rather,' he said to himself to confirm the picture.

It was a queer mixture of awe and romance, the alternation of his hatred for his own town and the love for the world to which he looked out. Men get used to a place, become familiar with it, and then comes a stage when the fascination of the unknown, the exotic, dominates them. It is the impulse which tries to create a new harmony, frowning upon the familiar which has grown stale and dreary with too much use. The mind which has once peeped into the wonderland of the new, contemplated various aspects of it with longing and desire, is shocked and disappointed when living reality pulls in the reins of the wild horse of fancy. But how pleasant men find it to look at the world with the open, hopeful, astonished eyes of the child! The vagaries of Bakha's naïve tastes can be both explained and excused. He didn't like his home, his street, his town, because he had been to work at the. Tommies' barracks, and obtained glimpses of another world, strange and beautiful; he had grown out of his native shoes into the ammunition boots that he had secured as a gift. And with this and other strange and exotic items of dress he had built up a new world, which was commendable, if for nothing else, because it represented a change from the old ossified order and the stagnating conventions of the life to which he was born. He was a pioneer in his own way, although he had never heard of that word, and was completely unconscious that it could be applied to him.

'What is the matter with you to-day?' asked Bakha's father, noticing the wild light in the boy's eyes and his listless manner. 'Are you tired?'

This started a panic in Bakha's soul. Should he tell or should he not? The sympathetic tone of the enquiry stirred the chords of his soul deeply. He could have wept at the apprehension implicit in his father's manner. He hesitated for a moment. Then, in a struggle to maintain the secret, he answered:

'Nothing,' he said, 'there is nothing.'

'Nothing! There is nothing!' echoed his father. 'Surely something is the matter. Come, tell the truth.'

Bakha felt he would break down and fall to pieces with his obstinate desire to suppress the secret. He was touched by the strange sympathy evinced by his father. He felt suffocated. He felt he couldn't sustain that mood for long. So he burst out with an explosion more sudden than the manner with which he was normally wont to utter a speech:

'They insulted me this morning, they abused me because as I was walking along a man happened to touch me. He gave me a blow. And a crowd gathered round me, abusing and—' He couldn't continue. He was possessed by an overpowering feeling of self-pity.

'My son,' said Lakha, with a forced mixture of anger and kindliness, 'didn't you give a warning of your approach?'

This burnt Bakha's soul. He sat tormented to think that he had told his father about his experience. 'I knew he would say that if I told him the truth,' he thought.

'Why weren't you more careful, my boy?' Lakha strained himself to be more kind than angry on noticing that his son was very agitated.

'But, father, what is the use?' Bakha shouted. 'They would ill-treat us even if we shouted. They think we are mere dirt because we clean their dirt. That pundit in the temple tried to molest Sohini and then came shouting: 'Polluted, polluted.' The woman of the big house in the silversmith's gulley threw the bread at me from the fourth story. I won't go down to the town again. I have done with this job.'

Lakha was touched. A queer self-conscious smile hovered on

the edges of his moustache, a smile of impotent rage.

'You didn't abuse or hit back, did you?' he asked. His sense of fear for his son for the consequences of such a crime, should he have been provoked to commit it, was mixed with that servile humility of his which could never entertain the prospect of retaliation against the high-caste men.

'No, but I was sorry afterwards that I didn't,' replied Bakha. 'I could have given them a bit of my mind.'

'No, no, my son, no,' said Lakha, 'we can't do that. They are our superiors. One word of theirs is sufficient to overbalance all that we might say before the police. They are our masters. We must respect them and do as they tell us. Some of them are kind.'

He looked at his son's face. It had relaxed a bit from the deliberate, tense expression it had assumed, to a sort of resigned cynicism, as if he didn't care. But the old man sensed that the boy was grieved and hurt, and he sensed also that he hated the high-caste people. He sought to assuage his son's grief, to placate his wrath.

'You know,' he began in the impersonal manner with which he always lifted himself from the lousy old man he was to the superior dignity of an aged father, 'You know, when you were a little child, I had a nasty experience too. You were ill with fever, and I went to the house of Hakim Bhagawan Das, in this very town. I shouted and shouted, but no one heard me. A babu was passing through the *Dawai Khana* (dispensary) of the Doctor and I said to him:

' "Babu ji, Babu ji, God will make you prosperous. Please make my message reach the ears of the Hakim ji. I have been shouting, shouting, and have even asked some people to tell the Hakim Sahib that I have a prayer to make to him. My child is suffering from fever. He has been unconscious since last night and I want the Hakim ji to give him some medicine."

' "Keep away, keep away," said the babu, "don't come riding on at me. Do you want me to have another bath this morning? The Hakim Sahib has to attend to us people who go to offices first, and there are so many of us waiting. You have nothing to do all day. Come another time or wait."

'And with this he walked into the dispensary.

'I remained standing. Whenever anyone passed by I would place my head at their feet and ask them to tell the Hakim. But who would listen to a sweeper? Everyone was concerned about himself.

'For an hour I stood like that in a corner, near the heap of litter which I had collected, and I was feeling as if a scorpion was stinging me. That I couldn't buy medicine for my son when I was willing to pay my hard-earned money for it, troubled me. I had seen many bottles full of medicine in the house of the Hakim ji and I knew that one of those bottles contained the medicine for you, and yet I couldn't get it. My heart was with you and my body was outside the house of the Hakim. I had torn my heart away from the room where you lay with your mother, and prayed to God to make my difficulty easy. But nothing happened. I began to think I was seeing you die. It seemed as if someone was giving me a blow in my side and saying "come and see the face of your son for the last time." I ran back home.

' "Have you brought the medicine?" asked your mother, rushing out to me.

'You, of course, only half opened your eyes and you were too delirious to recognise me. They told me they would soon bring you down on the floor.[1] So I ran back to the Hakim's house. Your mother shouted and said: "What is the good of medicine now?" But I ran and ran. When I got to the Hakim's house I just lifted the curtain and went straight in. I caught the Hakim's feet and said: 'Still there is a little breath left in my child's body, Hakim ji, I shall be your slave all my life. *The meaning of my life is my child.* Hakim ji, take pity. God will be kind to you."

---

[1]The Hindus do not allow a person to die in bed, but bring the dying to rest as near the earth as possible; the idea being that from the earth we come, to earth we return.

' "Bhangi! (Sweeper) Bhangi!" There was an uproar in the medicine house. People began to disperse hither and thither as the Hakim's feet had become defiled. He was red and pale in turn, and shouted at the highest pitch of his voice: 'Chandal! (low-caste) by whose orders have you come here? And then you join hands and hold my feet and say you will become my slave for ever. You have polluted hundreds of rupees worth of medicine. Will you pay for it?"

'I began to shed tears,' Lakha continued, 'and said: "Maharaj, Great One, I forgot. *Your shoe on my head.* I am not in my senses. Maharaj, you are my father and mother. I can't compensate for the medicines. I can only serve you. Will you come and give some medicine to my child? He is on his death-bed!"

'Hakim ji just shook his head and exclaimed: "Serve me! Serve me! How can you serve me? Have you ever received medicine here that you come rushing in?"

'I said: "Sarkar (Sir), I went away after standing outside for some time. I tried to fall at the feet of every passer-by and prayed them to tell to the Sarkar, your honour, that my child was suffering. But Sarkar, this is the time of kindness, be compassionate at this time, another time you can take even my life. Only save my child. All night I have been rocking him in my arms, thinking that if he survives the night, I shall come and fetch medicine from you with the rising of the sun. Who could have heard my call in the middle of the night if I had come here then?"

'With this the Hakim ji's heart melted to some extent and he began to write a prescription. Just at that time your uncle came running and shouted from without: "Ohe, Lakha! Ohe, Lakha! The boy is passing away!"

'I ran out. Hakim ji had dropped his pen. When I came home I found that you were very bad and they had put you on the floor for the fourth time, and your mother was crying.

'In a little while there was a knock at the door. And what do you think? Your uncle goes out and finds the Hakim ji himself, come to grace our house. He was a good man. He felt your pulse and saved your life.'

'He might have killed me,' Bakha commented.

'No, no,' said Lakha. 'They are really kind. We must realise that it is religion which prevents them from touching us.' He had never throughout his narrative renounced his deep-rooted sense of inferiority and the docile acceptance of the laws of fate.

Bakha had felt stirred in the deepest cells of his body as his father narrated the story. Every time his father mentioned his name, every time he referred to his dangerous illness, Bakha felt a strain of self-pity run through him which made him hot and cold at the same time, raised his hair on end and brought tears gushing to his eyes. It was by sheer exertion of his will power that he kept his weakness from actually letting the tears drop from his eyes. In a few moments, however, he was his own-strong self again.

'This rascal of a Rakha must have strayed away to play somewhere,' grumbled the old man. 'Whether you want to eat or not, I must. Sohini, give me some bread.'

'There is no salad,' said Sohini. 'Would you like to take it with some of the tea left over from the morning?'

'*What is taste to the palate of holy men, let it come with cream,*' the old man sang the familiar Indian proverb in reply. Sohini proceeded to put the smoke-bottomed handi full of tea-leaves, water and milk to boil.

Bakha crouched down to a tin jug and gingerly sprinkled a few drops of water on his hands and his face. He had heard his father ask for the food and he slightly resented it. 'I feel hungry too,' he thought. 'Perhaps much hungrier than he does. He has been sitting here all day.' The boy was, of course, too kind and self-sacrificing to believe that he grudged his old father the food that he was going to eat, but a feeling of disgust ran through him, the objection to the force of that biological expedient in him which, in its race across the stream of life, was sweeping everything out of its course. To the young and healthy animal in him, with the strength of his close-knit sinews, his old father was as good as dead. a putrefying corpse like that of a stray dog or cat on the rubbish-heap.

Rakha was at length in sight, a basket of food on his bare clean-shaven head, a pan slung by a string handle in his hand, and his feet dragging a pair of Bakha's old ammunition boots, laceless and noisy and too big for him. His tattered flannel shirt, grimy with the blowings of his ever-running nose, obstructed his walk slightly. The discomfort resulting from this, the fatigue, assumed or genuine, due to the work he had put in that morning, gave a rather drawn, long-jawed look to his dirty face on which the flies congregated in abundance to taste-of the sweet delights of the saliva on the corners of his lips. The quizzical, not-there look defined by his small eyes and his narrow, very narrow forehead, was positively ugly. And yet his ears, long and transparent in the sunlight, had something intelligent about them, something impish. He seemed a true child of the outcaste colony, where there are no drains, no light, no water; of the marshland where people live among the latrines of the townsmen, and in the stink of their own dung scattered about here, there and everywhere; of the world where the day is dark as the night and the night pitch-dark. He had wallowed in its mire, bathed in its marshes, played among its rubbish-heaps; his listless, lazy, lousy manner was a result of his surroundings. He was the vehicle of a life-force, the culminating point in the destiny of which would never come, because malaria lingered in his bones, and that disease does not kill but merely dissipates the energy. He was a friend of the flies and the mosquitoes, their boon companion since his childhood.

'So you have got back after all,' Bakha exclaimed when Rakha was within hearing distance.

His younger brother did not reply, but came sulkily up to where Sohini sat in the kitchen and, depositing his loads of food before her, sat down in the dust, exploring the heap of crumbs in his basket. He ate big morsels. His mouth filled on one side. It looked grotesque.

'At least wash your hands, you wild animal!' said Bakha, irritated by the sight of his brother's running nose.

'You mind your own business,' retorted the young boy as if

he based his defence on the solid foundation of his superior moral force, which indeed he did, because he knew his father sat on the bed, the person who loved him more than he loved Bakha.

'Look at yourself in the mirror! What a picture you look!' exclaimed Bakha.

'Don't keep on finding fault with him,' put in Lakha. 'Stop quarrelling, occasionally, at least.'

'Come and eat a piece of bread,' said Sohini to her elder brother sympathetically.

Bakha got up from his chair unwillingly and, crouching by the kitchen, casually dipped his hand in the basket. There was a heap of food there, broken pieces of chapatis, some whole ones and lentil curry in a bowl.

They all ate from the same basket and the same bowl, not apportioning the food in different plates as the Hindus do, for the original Hindu instinct for cleanliness had disappeared long ago. Only Bakha felt a thrill of loathing go through him for his brother after he had eaten his first few morsels of the day. He changed his position slightly, so that he had his back turned towards his brother. But his hand touched a piece of sticky, wet bread. He shrank back from the basket. The picture of a sepoy washing his hands in his round brass tray, over the leavings of bread and salad, and then throwing them in Rakha's basket appeared before him. He had himself gone so often to beg for food and the only thing he hated about it was the sight of those bits of bread softened by the water poured upon them. He had a queer warm feeling of water running under his tongue from across the sides of his mouth. He felt sick. He tried to drop the soft crumb he had got hold of, but some of it stuck to his fingers still. It was nauseating. He rose from the floor.

'You were saying you were hungry!' said Lakha, when he saw his son get up so suddenly from the meal.

Bakha bent over the tin vessel from the mouth of which he was sprinkling drops of water on his hand. He didn't know what to say in reply. 'He won't understand if I tell him that I feel

sick,' he said to himself. 'I will make an excuse. But what—'
Suddenly a pretence occurred to him.

'I have to go to Ram Charan's house to see his sister's
marriage—and to receive my share of the sweets,' he said. The
last he added tactfully, to fortify himself against any objection his
father might have to his going, by appealing to the old man's
greed.

The true reason for the sudden impulse that had come so
usefully in the invention of his lie was inexplicable to anyone,
even to himself. For even he did not realise why he was going
to see the wedding of Ram Charan's sister. He hadn't been
invited to go by Gulabo (of course he could not have been invited
by her, quarrelsome as she was, abusing even such a docile
person as Bakha for one thing or another, especially for his
encouraging her son to truancy) or by Ram Charan. And he
couldn't have been asked by Ram Charan's sister, because she
had never talked to him since she was ten. Why then was he
going? What had made him decide so suddenly on such an
extraordinary adventure?

He only knew that he wanted to get away from home, his
father, his brother, his sister, everyone. But he wouldn't confess
even to himself that he was going to see Ram Charan's sister for
the last time. A picture of her appeared from the past before his
mind's eye. She was a tiny girl with shaven head, wearing a
miniature skirt of gaudy red cotton with a white pattern, that the
washerwomen wear. She looked like a juggler's little monkey. He
himself was then a boy of eight, in a gold-embroidered cap which
his father had begged from a moneylender who had three small
sons whose discarded clothes fitted Lakha's three children exactly.
Bakha remembered how, while he had been playing with her
brother and Chota in the barracks, they had come home and
started to play at marriage. Ram Charan's little sister was made
to act the wife because she wore a skirt. Bakha was chosen to
play the husband because he was wearing the gold-embroidered

cap. The rest of the boys took the part of members of the marriage party. Bakha recalled how he had been ragged by Chota for acting as the husband of a shaven-headed, ridiculous little girl, and how he (Bakha) had been angry with him, although he himself thought she looked funny. There was something wistful about her, a soft light in her eyes, for which she had become endeared to him and for which, he, remembered, he had actually quarrelled with his friend. Since then, of course, she had grown up to be a tall girl with a face as brown as ripe wheat and hair as black as the rain clouds. And Bakha always felt proud of having once acted as her husband. Being very reticent and shy, however, he seldom dared even to look at her. But in the depths of his being he had felt waves of confusion at the thought of her. Now at the age of fourteen she was being married off to a young washerman attached as a follower to the 31st Punjabis regiment. He had heard of this arrangement a year ago. It was common knowledge in the sweepers' street that Gulabo had taken two hundred rupees for the hand of her daughter. Chota had told him that. He remembered the evening on which he had heard it, for it had been somewhat of a shock to him, and he had felt a regret in his soul, as if a spring of water had burst like a doleful lyric melody in the hard rock of his body. During the dreary hours of his routine work at the latrines, subsequently, he had often heard the delicate strain of that sad, elfin music. But he had never quite comprehended the source from which it came. In the darkness of his home at night, when he lay half asleep, something in him secretly led him towards the vague sylph-like form which he could have squeezed in the embrace of his arms, and still he could not connect the feelings he had at such moments with the ripples that surged up in him whenever he caught sight of Ram Charan's sister.

As he walked towards her home to-day, however, he recalled occasions on which his vague flowings towards her had become more defined. His large eyes had rested with adoration on her face as she met him once going to the shops to buy some kerosene oil in an old wine-bottle. Then from the dark undeclared places of his soul arose another picture of her in his memory— as she came through the darkness before the dawn from the banks of the brook where, he knew, she and the other women of the outcastes' colony went every day, taking advantage of the privacy which the half-light afforded, to perform their toilets unseen by men. He remembered that he had been about the latrines and had at first felt a thrill of delight, then a sensation more vital. He had pictured her quite naked as he had seen his mother quite often when he was a child, and his sister, and other little children. An impulse had arisen like a sudden gust of wind to his brain, and darkened his thoughts. He had felt as if he could forcibly gather the girl in his embrace and ravish her. Then he had put his hand across his eyes and shuddered in horror at the thought. He had cursed himself for such a vision. His reputation as a docile, good, respectable boy seemed at stake. He had wondered at himself: 'How could I, who am known to, everyone as Bakha the good, have such an unholy design?' Nevertheless, the picture had persisted. The more he tried to blot it out, the more definite it had become, until, when he had ceased to bother about his sensual feelings, his phantasy had vanished.

As he recalled these things, he seemed to feel ashamed. He had felt that shame also on the occasion when those things first happened. In a frantic effort to escape from himself, to escape from the secret, buried desire he had for the girl, he casually took a turning off the track which led to the washermen's houses, and wandered aimlessly into a lane which ended in the washermen's ghats by the waterside.

Shioh! Shioh! Shi! A few washermen were shouting as they tore the garments of their customers and broke their buttons on slabs of stone by the edges of the brook. Their dark legs were immersed in the water up to the knee and their bodies from the rumps upwards were swathed in the thick folds of loin-cloths up to the waists, where their shirts were tucked in. They doubled over the stones with supple movements and struck the garments with a loud swinging sweep which was graceful in itself even if it did not do any good to the cloth. Bakha had often stood watching this operation. In his childhood, of course, he had been fascinated by it, so that he wished to become a washerman. It was Ram Charan, true son of his mother, Gulabo, if he, wasn't his father's son, but of the rich man, his mother's lover, who had knocked the bottom out of that ambition by telling Bakha that though he (Ram Charan) touched him and played with him, he was a Hindu, while Bakha was a mere sweeper. Bakha was too young then to understand the distinction implied in the washer-boy's arrogant claim, or else he would have slapped Ram Charan's face. But now he knew that there were degrees of castes among the low-caste, and that he was of the lowest.

He looked hard among the few washermen who beat clothes upon the slabs of stone. He anxiously explored among the stray washermen's donkeys which grazed on the side of the brook, wildly thinking that Ram Charan might be there. He looked across the yards of space on which the washed, wet clothes lay drying in the hot afternoon sun. But he was looking in vain. For how could Ram Charan have absented himself from so auspicious an occasion as his sister's marriage and be working here! 'Only, did Ram Charan not absent himself at the time of his father's death and go fishing with us?' Bakha thought. 'He might be here to-day.' Then he thought: 'Perhaps his father wasn't his father, but he is his sister's brother. I will have to go to his place after all.'

He began to walk back. He felt shy. He didn't know how he could approach the house where festivities were going on. 'All the members of the washermen's brotherhood will be there, dressed in their best clothes, singing strange southern music. How shall I be able to stand there and look?' He felt ashamed to picture the scene. He was highly strung to-day. A strange leprosy seemed to have struck his tissues, his vertebrae seemed to be eaten up from within. 'How shall I be able to call Ram Charan when I get there?' he said.

Between the intervals of wiping the sweat off his brow, his ordinary self came back. The nervousness descended into the crowded world of his entrails, leaving the surface of his mind clean like a slate. He got to the kerb of the outcastes' street and stopped still, suddenly, within ten yards of Ram Charan's house. He had the pleasantest surprise. Chota stood, leaning by a wooden pillar, staring with wonder at the crowd of men and women gathered in the one-roomed mud-house and outside on the veranda.

Bakha advanced gingerly towards the wooden pillar and came and stood by Chota. His friend turned with surprise at him and cordially pressed him by the hand. Then they both fell to staring at the dazed, happy crowd before them. Bakha noticed how white the starched linen, which the washermen wore, seemed against their black skins. At first, however, he could not concentrate his gaze on the individuals. He felt afraid to lift his eyes beyond the veranda to the cavernous room scarcely illuminated by the glowing sun outside. A wave of warmth descended down the back of his head. Through the haze he could see a man from within looking at him. He felt quivers of self-consciousness pass through him. The thought of Ram Charan's sister came into collision with the sight of her. His heart sank within him. He was sweating. Luckily for him, the double beat of a drum tore the air and lifted all the confusion in Bakha's soul on the flapping, hovering wings of the song that accompanied it. It was a queer refrain, sudden as thunder, as it ranged over three notes of the minor scale, sung in unison by the whole assembly. In the very beginning it was a shrill wail, which went through the tympanum of the ear to the head, and seemed to make the listener mad with its ever-sharpening frenzy, as lightning which pokes its sharp spears of power through the head and leaves it athrob. Before they proceeded very far, the song had mounted above the drum and established the reign of an exhilarating rhythm. Bakha floated on the strain as he might have done on a swing. Then as the melody arose steeply to its full height of enthusiasm in the swaying, rolling, rocking, yelling frames of the washermen and washerwomen, Bakha again felt cold and impassive with self-consciousness. He touched Chota's arm nervously, hiding his movement in the blaze of riotous excess to which the washermen had carried their song. Chota greeted him with a broad grin as cordial as the contagious spirit of happiness in the atmosphere could make it.

'I shall call Ram Charan,' said Chota, and quite unafraid and unashamed to face the crowd of singing washermen he called Ram Charan, who sat dressed in a rather contradictory style of Eastern and Western habiliments—a large khaki topee on his small head, a muslin shirt, clean and white, but torn near the collar, and a pair of shorts on his thin, bare black legs.

At first Ram Charan was too absorbed, eating the *ludus* (sugar-plums) which his mother was distributing with the tankards of native wine, for Chota's message to pass from the washerman near him to whom he had entrusted it, through the forest of heads, to Ram Charan. Then luckily for his friends, as Ram Charan stood up to sprinkle the red colour over the white clothes of the crowd through a crude spray made out of a tin can, the ceremonial little mischief-maker was lifted amid the happy cries and shouts of hilarious laughter of the white-clad men, now spotted profusely with scarlet, and thrown out.

'Come,' he greeted Chota and Bakha, blinking his lashless eyes, and ran ahead.

'Give, o bey brother-in-law, give us some of the sweets,' said Chota.

Ram Charan had not forgotten to fill the pockets of his shorts, and his large silk handkerchief, stolen from the laundry bag of some rich merchant, with sugar-plums.

'Keep quiet for a while,' said Ram Charan, suddenly turning back to see if his mother was aware of the direction he was going to take.

She was.

'Oh, you illegally begotten!' came her voice shrilly, audible above all the other noises. 'Are you running away to play with that dirty sweeper and leather-worker on the very day of your sister's marriage? You ought to be ashamed of yourself, you little dog!'

'Shut up, you bitch!' replied Ram Charan, as was his wont, for he had been hardened into an impudent, obstinate young rascal by the persistency of his mother's abuse. And with Chota at his heels and Bakha following clumsily behind, he led the way towards the heath which sloped gently towards the north of the outcastes' colony.

'Give us some of those sugar-plums, brother-in-law!' insisted Chota, greedy and gay. 'I have waited for an hour for you outside your noisy house.'

'You shall have some as soon as we get to the hill,' assured Ram Charan. 'I have brought them for you and Bakha, not for anyone else. Now let us run, for my mother might come after me.' And he carried himself with the assurance of one who has suddenly come into power. Chota at least, if not Bakha, paid him the homage which he expected as his due because he had a dozen sugar-plums in his possession.

'Come, O elephant,' he rebuked Bakha for his coldness, 'show your teeth and lift your legs. You shall have some sweets soon.'

Bakha dismissed the impudence of his joke with a grunt and followed quietly. He was feeling quite detached from the human world, swathed in a sort of unadulterated melancholy.

The hand of nature was stretching itself out towards him, for the tall grass on the slopes of Bulashah Hills was in sight, and he had opened his heart to it, lifted by the cool breeze that wafted him away from the crowds, the ugliness and the noise of the outcastes' street. He looked across at the swaying loveliness before him and the little hillocks over which it spread under a sunny sky, so transcendingly blue and beautiful that he felt like standing dumb and motionless before it. He listened to the incoherent whistling of the shrubs. They were the voices he knew so well. He was glad that his friends were ahead of him and that the thrum was not broken, for the curve of his soul seemed to bend over the heights, straining to woo nature in solitude and silence. It seemed to him he would be unhappy if he heard even one human voice. His inside seemed to know that it wouldn't be soothed if there were the slightest obstruction between him and the outer world. It didn't even occur to him to ask why he had come here. He was just swamped by the merest fringe of the magnificent fields that spread before him. He. had been startled into an awareness of the mystery of vegetable moods.

As he rambled along, however, he felt he wanted an adventure in friendship to humanise the solitary excursion of the stoic in him. But he didn't want to call Ram Charan, or Chota, to come and share his joy with him. He fell back to a memory of the adventures he had had here in his childhood. He remembered the time in his early days when he used to come to the heath with all the other boys, to fight battles for the imaginary fort they had built by fixing a flag on the top of the hill. The bamboo bows with which they flung arrows at each other came before him and the imitation toy pistols with their sparks. How enthusiastic all the boys used to feel about him then! They had made him their *Jernel* (general). He recalled with pride the pitched battle they had fought against the boys of the 28th Sikhs and won. They were helter-skelter battles, not quite like the organised manoeuvres of the regiments, fought with guns. 'But then,' he said to himself, 'they were the games played in childhood. I wouldn't play those games now. I can hardly spare time to play hockey, with my father shouting at me all the time.' He felt a bit lonely thinking such thoughts. He switched his mind on to the landscape in that vague groping manner in which his mind always felt its way across things. On the slopes, carpeted with grass, there flourished a wilderness of flowers, of which the shades changed at various intervals. There were the yellow buttercups, which had seemed to Bakha always like the mustard-seed flower of his village near

Sialkot; then there were the long-stalked, single-headed daisies, alternating with grades of purple and white anemones—to Bakha all flowers, mere flowers, for he didn't know their names. A pool of water in long grass and ferns looked like a large basin round which the silver birches bent down and, smitten by the wind, seemed to be drinking. Here every passer-by quenched his thirst from the water that sprang from a natural spring.

Descending down to it, with his nostrils full of fresh air, and his heart as light as the spirits of the sparrows which chirped, Bakha seemed nevertheless unaroused and unresponsive as a child turning aside from every wayside flower, for though he had the receptivity of the man who is willing to lend his senses to experience, he had an unenlightened will. Necessity had forced him to the contemplation of the charms of nature, merely superficially. Heredity had furrowed no deep grooves in his soul where flowers could grow or grass abound. The cumulative influence of careful selection had imprisoned, his free will in the shackles of slavery to the dreary routine of one occupational environment. He could not reach out from the narrow and limited personality he had inherited to his larger yearning. It was a discord between person and circumstance by which a lion like him lay enmeshed in a net while many a common criminal wore a rajah's crown. His wealth of unconscious experience, however, was extraordinary. It was a kind of crude sense of the world, in the round, such as the peasant who can do the job has, while the laboratory agriculturalist is scratching his head, or like the Arab seaman who sails the seas in a small boat and casually determines his direction by the position of the sun, or like the beggar singer who recites an epic from door to door. But it wanted the force and vivacity of thought to transmute his vague sense into the superior instinct of the *really* civilised man.

As he sauntered along a spark of some intuition suddenly set him ablaze. He was fired with a desire to burst out from the shadow of silence and obscurity in which he lay enshrouded.

He rushed down to the slope, towards the trees that stood by the pool below him. The soft breeze came whispering up to him and made his blood tingle with its soft, fresh coolness. The sun on the curve of the sky before him was being reflected from the sheen of the rippling water with a restlessness like the pain in Bakha's soul. He descended through the meadows, rank with herbage, before he had breathed more than a breath. He lay down on the bank of the pool and immediately lent himself to the stillness about him, making not the slightest stir, even though the position in which he leaned back exposed his eyes uncomfortably to the sun. In a moment or two his frame seemed to have sunk into insignificance, drowned as it were in a pit of silence, while the things on the sunny bank began to take life, each little stem of plant becoming a big leaf, distinct and important. The whole valley seemed to him aglow with life.

But the rich and exuberant spaces about him seemed to have sucked all his energy away. He lay as if dead. His empty belly had provoked the subtle urgings of sleep into play. He was dozing.

He had hardly dozed off before Chota came and began to tickle his nose with a straw. With one wild sneeze the sweeper-lad got up and sat with his trunk upright in the face of his friends' double-barrelled laughter. Bakha was no killjoy to be annoyed by so ordinary a practical joke and willingly let himself be made a fool of. But the incidents of the morning had cast a shadow over him and there was something forced in his smile as against the spontaneous heartiness of his companions. Chota noticed this. He saw that there, was something tense about it, something accusing, as if Bakha really disapproved of the joke which had been played on him.

'What is the matter with you, brother-in-law?' he asked.

'Nothing,' replied Bakha. 'You were running. I came slowly.'

'You didn't look for us?'

'I was tired. I wanted to sleep. I couldn't sleep very well last night.'

'Because you will be a gentreman and won't put a quilt over you as your father says,' joked Chota. He learnt from Rakha all that happened to Bakha at home, all the abuse that their father inflicted upon him, and he used to tease him about it.

'Shut up,' retorted Bakha playfully, 'you are more of a gentreman than I am, and look at this brother-in-law to-day; he is wearing a sahib's topee and shorts.'

Although they all aspired to copy English customs, they were not altogether unconscious of the falseness of their instinct, and could see the edge of their elders' sarcastic reproach: '*Look at this gentreman!*' and repeated it amongst each other.

'What about those sugar-plums?' Bakha continued, referring to Ram Charan. He wasn't particularly keen to have them although he would have liked to eat one.

'Here is your portion,' said Ram Charan, unfolding the handkerchief which he carried.

There were three sugar-plums in it, all slightly broken.

'Throw me one,' said Bakha.

'Take it,' said Ram Charan.

But Bakha hesitated and didn't hold his hands out.

'Take it, why don't you take it?' Ram Charan grumbled.

'No, give it to me, throw it,' Bakha said.

Both Ram Charan and Chota were surprised. Never before had they seen Bakha behave like that. Ram Charan was admitted to be of the higher caste among them, because he was a washerman. Chota, the leather-worker's son, came next in the hierarchy, and Bakha was of the third and lowest category. But among the trio they had banished all thought of distinction, except when the snobbery of caste feeling supplied the basis for putting on airs for a joke. They had eaten together, if not of things in the preparation of which water had been used, at least dry things, this being in imitation of the line drawn by the Hindus between themselves and the Mohammedans and Christians. Sweets they had often shared together, and they had handled soda-water bottles anyhow, at all those formal hockey matches they played once a year, with the boys' teams of the various regiments in the Bulashah Brigade.

'What has happened to you?' queried Chota in a voice full of deep concern, and then he added caressingly: 'Come, friend, tell us.'

'Nothing, it's nothing,' said Bakha.

'Come, come, we are your friends,' implored Chota.

Bakha told them how when he left them that morning he was walking through the town, a man happened to brush past him, and how he began to abuse him, and summoned a large crowd; and how before he could get away, he had slapped him.

'Why didn't you strike back?' Chota asked, enraged.

'That wasn't the only thing,' continued Bakha. And he narrated how the priest tried to molest his sister and then came shouting at them both: 'Polluted, polluted.'

'You wait till the illegally begotten comes to our street side. We will skin the fellow,' shouted Chota indignantly.

'There was another insult waiting for me further up,' Bakha added, and he narrated the story of how the woman in the silversmith's alley had flung the bread down at him from the top of her house.

'Comrade, we're sorry,' assured Chota. 'Come, be brave, forget all this. What can we do? We are outcastes.' He patted Bakha comfortingly. 'Come,' he consoled again, 'forget all about it. We will go and play hockey. Let that *brother-in-law* of a priest come down our street, and we will teach him the lesson of his life.'

'Come, let's go,' put in Ram Charan, who was slightly embarrassed by Bakha's narrative, and growingly afraid that his mother would curse him if he absented himself from home too long. 'I'll have to put in an appearance at home before I can come and play hockey,' he said, looking from Chota to Bakha.

'Come,' urged Chota soothingly, with a deep strain of melancholy in his voice.

Bakha got to his feet and the three of them began to walk quietly homewards.

Ram Charan was beginning to feel very embarrassed by the silence, so embarrassed that he thought it no fit occasion to remain adorned with such a symbol of greatness as his solar hat. So he lifted his strange, large headgear off its small, uneasy seat and followed sheepishly.

Bakha's soul seemed to lie bare before his friends, bruised and tender. Chota felt with him. He allied himself with Bakha's mood.

The sympathy that the repetition of his narrative evoked from his friends accentuated Bakha's self-pity. He began, as he walked along, to feel the heart-burnings of the morning. He felt furious, his fury heightening with the invisible strength that the presence of his two friends gave him. 'Chota and I could teach that immoral wretch of a Brahmin a lesson,' he reflected.

'What do you say to our catching hold of the swine one day?' put in Chota.

This is strange, Bakha felt, that Chota should think of the same thing at the same time as I. But he felt unequal to the suggestion as he felt unequal to his own desire.

'What is the use?' he replied, sighing. He didn't want to refuse to wreak his vengeance too openly. And then he felt sad and pensive, because he couldn't rise to the realisation of his own urges. He resolved to tighten himself. He gnashed his teeth. A warmth rose to his ears. He felt a quickening in his blood. Then came the sweep of his ever-recurring emotions. He boiled with rage. 'Horrible, horrible,' his soul seemed to cry out within him. He felt the most excruciating mental pain he had ever felt in his body. He shivered. His broad, impassive face was pale with hostility. But he couldn't do anything. He hung his head and walked with a drooping chest. His frame seemed to be burdened with the weight of an inexpressible, unrelieved power. He was deliberately trying to hide his stature in his stoop, as if he were afraid of being seen at all.

'Where is that brother-in-law, Ram Charan?' said Chota to relieve the tension.

'Looking for mushrooms,' Bakha joked. With this his knitted brows relaxed and his furrowed forehead became uncreased. The cowed defiance of his manner gave place to an easy, natural air. He was absorbed in the spectacle of the town of Bulashah sleeping snugly in the afternoon hush at the foot of the hill. From the clump of trees, visible beyond the distant north gate, to the cantonment in the south, from the mango groves in the east to the little group of houses of the outcastes' colony, the white-blue lower sky was defined into a lovely pattern by the golden domes of the temples, the flat roofs of the houses and the carved terraces with big blue clay flower-pots fixed to their sides. And then the thatched hut of his home in the swamps and shallows presented itself to his gaze. The contrast of the tremulous line of foliage which lay near him and beyond, the green, green mango orchards and the marshland which surrounded his home, was a stark one.

'I think I shall also go and show my face at home before I come to play hockey,' said Chota suddenly. 'There is too much sunshine yet.'

'All right, Havildar Charat Singh said he would give me a hockey stick if I called this afternoon,' Bakha said, 'I shall go and get it.'

'All right, you go and get the stick,' agreed Chota. 'Charan and I will join you before the match begins. Meanwhile we shall take this footpath.'

They had reached a small lane which led to the outcastes' colony through cactus hedges. They branched off.

Bakha strode along in the open through the stones in the old river-bed that stretched itself between the hills and the barracks of the 38th Dogras. He felt that he had just invented this business with Charat Singh because he didn't want to go home, because he didn't want to see his father, his brother, his sister, because he didn't want to go and work at the latrines—at least, not to-day. For a moment he felt a compunction that he was trying to escape. But he had grown out of his surroundings and he just hated the thought of being in the neighbourhood of his mud-house.

Somewhere in him he felt he could never get away from it, but to the greater part of him the place didn't exist. It had been effaced clean off the map of his being.

There was not a soul to be seen about in the compound of the barracks. Even the quarter-guard seemed empty and forlorn, except for the two dummy-like sentries who walked up and down the veranda outside the magazine which Bakha knew to be behind the locked doors. Only a solar topee seemed to Bakha alive, instinct'with life, there, as it hung on the wall. There were many legends current about this hat. Some said it was a symbol of authority of the *sahib logs* (white men) who ruled over the regiment. Others said that the hat had been forgotten in the regimental office by a sahib (officer) once, and since, being a sahib (rich man), he didn't care to reclaim his lost property, it had been kept on at the quarter-guard. Again, it was rumoured that a sahib had once been court-martialled for shooting a sepoy, and since he was a white man and could never be put behind the bars in the lock-up at the quarterguard, his hat and belt and sword had been imprisoned instead. The sahib had suddenly disappeared. Some people said he had been helped by the officer commanding the regiment to escape overnight in order to evade the sentence of imprisonment pronounced by the judges, and only the hat had remained at the quarter-guard. If, on the other hand, you asked one of the sentries whose hat it was, they always told you it belonged to a sahib (an officer) who had just gone into the grounds and would be soon returning to take it. But nobody ever asked questions about this hat except the children of the 38th Dogras. The younger among these children believed what the sentries said and ran away, for great was the fear attaching to the persons of the sahibs, like the dread of pale-white ghosts, ghouls and hobgoblins, because they were rumoured to be very irritable, liable to strike you with their canes if you looked at them. The elder boys knew it was a lie invented by the sentries to drive the curious little boys away, as they remembered having seen that hat for years in the same place, and realised it couldn't have been just left there by a sahib every time they saw it.

But even they didn't really know why the sentries invented the lie. They didn't realise that the sepoys too wanted the hat, not because they could wear it, either with their uniform or their mufti, but because they thought of the wonder it would arouse in the hills at home, the interest it would arouse among the villagers. People would come to see it for miles, as they came to see their *vardi* (uniform) and their white clothes, with ogling eyes and admiring glances. How proud, they thought, they would feel carrying this symbol of Sahibhood in their luggage, going home to Kangra or Hoshiarpur.

But why had all these stories about the solar hat got round? Because there wasn't a child about the 38th Dogras who hadn't cast lingering eyes at this hat. The spirit of modernity had worked havoc among the youth of the regiment. The consciousness of every child was full of a desire to wear Western dress, and since most of the boys about the place were the sons of babus, bandsmen, sepoys, sweepers, washermen and shopkeepers, all too poor to afrord the luxury of a complete European outfit, they eagerly stretched their hands to seize any particular article they could see anywhere, feeling that the possession of something European was better than the possession of nothing European. A hat with its curious distinction of shape and form, with the peculiar quality of honour that it presents to the Indian eye because it adorns the noblest part of the body, had a fascination such as no other item of European dress possessed.

Bakha had for years looked with longing at the solar topee that hung on the peg in the veranda of the 38th Dogras' quarter-guard. Ever since he was a little child he had contemplated it with the wonder-struck gaze of the lover and the devotee. Whenever he was given the chance of going out sweeping in the compounds of the 38th Dogras' barracks, he invariably chose the quarter-guard side, for there he could steal glances at the object he coveted, and plan various devices to win it. Those were nice thoughts, those connected with the schemes he concocted in order to possess that hat.

One of the ways in which it could be acquired, he had thought, was to make friends with one of the non-commissioned officers in charge of the quarter-guard. But it was impracticable. There was never the same non-commissioned officer in charge of the quarter-guard for two days and nights together. The guard changed every twelve hours, and considering it was one N.C.O. from one of the many platoons of one of the twelve companies in the regiment, you could never hope to see the same non-commissioned officer at the quarter-guard twice in your life.

That scheme failing, Bakha had thought of asking one of the sentries. When he was a child he had once dared to do that, but then the sentry had sent him away with the yarn about the sahib who had left it for a moment while he was in the grounds, and who would soon come back to get it. Now, however, he dared not ask. Some of the sepoys gave themselves such airs. 'They might abuse me,' he said to himself. 'Better any time to ask a Havildar. Every Havildar is an experienced person with long service and surely knows my father, the Jemadar of the sweepers. He will be kind even if he doesn't actually give me the hat.' But he could not bring himself to ask, he just couldn't. 'Why is it,' he had often asked himself, 'that I can't go and ask now but dared to do so when I was a child?' He couldn't find the answer to this. He didn't know that with the growth of years he had lost the freedom, the wild, careless, dauntless freedom of the child, that he had lost his courage, that he was afraid.

Then he deceived himself by believing that he didn't really want the hat, because he could get any number of them at the rag shop or from some Tommy in the British barracks. But he still longed for the hat. For years he had pined for it. And now he stood contemplating it with the same interest, the same curiosity, the same desire to possess it, with which he had looked at it during these years. It was not too clean a topee. The dust of years had settled on it. The khaki cloth-cover, with the quilt-like pattern, had faded to a dirty white, and, of course, no one knew what it was like inside.

Bakha stared at it hard, as he stood in a corner of the quarter-guard off the track where the sentries paraded to and fro. It didn't seem to move any nearer towards him. 'What can I do?' he asked himself. 'Go and ask that sentry,' his mind told him. 'But no, he might not understand,' the doubt arose, 'he might not understand what I am talking about if I, a sweeper, suddenly put it to him that I want the hat. He looks rather stern. There is no chance of getting near him.'

He looked round to see if there were anyone else about. There wasn't a soul. He guessed that everyone was having a siesta. He felt an irresistible desire to go and steal the hat. If only that sentry was not there. 'One could do it,' he thought, 'when the sentry turns his face away and walks to the other end of his beat. But someone might come and surprise me. It is too big a thing, this hat, to conceal. Besides if I stole it, I could never wear it. Everyone in the regiment knows about it. No, it is impossible. No, there is no way of getting it.' Once more he cast a loving glance at it and walked away towards the barracks at the nearer end of which, he knew, lived Havildar Charat Singh.

It wasn't far. A hundred yards or so. The time involved in covering this space Bakha occupied with a picture of himself playing hockey with the solar topee on. He saw himself running about in it. How important he looked, the idol of all the boys. Then it occurred to him that solar topees are not worn at hockey. 'How foolish my thoughts are,' he said. He was slightly ashamed of his predilection in favour of English dress, but he derived consolation from the fact that he had never made such a fool of himself as Ram Charan did by wearing a hat and shorts at his sister's marriage.

He crossed through a ditch and was in sight of the long rows of barracks. The particular one he wanted was only ten yards ahead of him. It had a long veranda. He reached the room at the near end of it. That was Havildar Charat Singh's place. He walked past it, because he was embarrassed. He was always ashamed of being seen. He felt like a thief. Luckily for his self-consciousness, the door of the room was shut. There was no way for him to know whether the Havildar was at home. An ordinary person could go and shout for the Havildar, or could go and strike the latch. He was a sweeper and dared not go within defiling distance of the veranda. Bakha wished that the system which the Emperor Jehangir had invented, if the story of the babu's son was right, now prevailed, of a bell in the Emperor's house which was attached to a string at the outer gates and by the pulling of which the King could be informed of the applicants waiting for admission. He had to shout for his food in the town. He had no way of getting into touch with Ram Charan or Chota when he went to their houses except by shouting, and that meant Ram Charan's mother and Chota's father recognising his voice, and shouting back abusively at him for trying to seduce their sons to play truant. And now, of course, he couldn't shout or do anything. The Havildar might be asleep. The sepoys might be having their siesta too. And they would be disturbed.

He walked to and fro outside the veranda. Then he lay down under a tree. His thoughts began to drift. 'I don't know what I can do. I hope he remembers the promise he made this morning. Otherwise all this time will be wasted for nothing. My father must be cursing me. I haven't worked all the afternoon. But never mind. Let Rakha do it for a change. I have been doing it all this while. What if I take an afternoon off?' His eyes drifted to the kitchen where the food for Charat Singh's company was cooked. He remembered he had been there quite often to get food when he was a child, when his father was attached to 'B' company as an ordinary sweeper. The figures of the hockey-playing members of this company passed through his mind. There was Hoshiar Singh, who played centre-half, the pivot of the team. There was Lekh Ram, who played centre-forward. There was Shiv Singh, who played right full-back. And, of course, there was the redoubtable Charat Singh, who kept goal. He recalled the story current about Charat Singh, that the days he didn't spend playing hockey he spent in hospital, suffering from the wounds and bruises he received playing hockey. He could picture the man keeping goal in the matches against the British regiment. He always stood leaning by the goalpost till the ball came his way and he just fell upon it. The number of scars he had on his body equalled in number, said the babu's son, the marks of sword and lance on the body of the Rajput warrior Rana Sanga, the conqueror of Akbar, the great Moghul. And the most delightful of the injuries which he had ever sustained was to have had his teeth knocked out, for he had had them replaced with a row of false ones, mounted with gold, which had led to many a joke, when someone ingeniously suggested that the proverb 'A straw in the beard of a thief' should be changed to 'Gold teeth in the mouth of the thief.'

Bakha had not fully given himself up to his reverie when he saw Charat Singh come out of his door, brass jug in hand. The Havildar sat down on the veranda profusely splashing water into his eyes and on his face. Too absorbed in his toilet and still half asleep, he didn't notice Bakha sitting under the *Kikir* tree. The sweeper-boy got up with a half-embarrassed, half-daring look, and lifting his hand to his brow, said: 'Salaam, Havildar ji.'

'Come, ohe Bakhia, how are you?' said Charat Singh enthusiastically. 'I have not seen you about at the regimental hockey matches lately. Where do you keep yourself hidden?'

'I have to work, Havildar ji,' Bakha replied.

'Oh, work, work, blow work!' exclaimed Charat Singh, forgetful in the manifestation of his present goodwill that he had himself shouted at Bakha for neglecting his work that morning.

Bakha was conscious of this anomaly. But he was altogether too favourably inclined towards Charat Singh to let anything stand in the way of his admiration for the hockey hero. There was a comfortable, homely glow radiating from the smile that the Havildar wore. Bakha felt happy in his presence. 'For this man,' he said to himself, 'I wouldn't mind being a sweeper all my life. I would do anything for him.'

Charat Singh got up and wiped his face with the edge of his coarse homespun loin-cloth. Then he picked up a little hookah with a coco-nut shell for a water-basin, and a delicately-carved marionette-like stem crowned by a red clay basin for charcoal and tobacco. He separated the earthen pot from the neck of the hubble-bubble and said to Bakha:

'Go and get me two pieces of coal from the kitchen.'

The boy stood wonder-struck. That a Hindu should entrust him with the job of fetching glowing charcoal in the chilm which he was going to put on his hookah and smoke! For a moment he looked as if an electric shock had passed through him. Then the strange suggestion produced a pleasant thrill in his being; it exhilarated him. He took the chilm from Charat Singh and, wrapped in an atmosphere of delight, walked towards the kitchen fifty yards away.

'Call the cook also to me,' shouted Charat Singh after him, 'and tell him to bring my tea.'

'Very good, Havildar ji,' said Bakha, and walked away without looking back, lest he should prove unequal to the unique honour that the Hindu had done him by entrusting him with so intimate a job as fetching coal in his clay basin. 'What? Is it wet or dry?' he asked himself. 'Could it be defiled, I wonder?' The answer came back to him: 'Oh, yes, the tobacco is wet. Of course it could be defiled.' For a moment he doubted whether Charat Singh was conscious and in his senses when he entrusted him with the job. 'He might be forgetful and suddenly realise what he had done. Did he forget that I am a sweeper? He couldn't have done, I was just talking to him about my work. And he saw me this morning. How could he have forgotten?' Thus reassured he was grateful to God that such men as Charat Singh existed. He walked with a steady step, with a happy step, deliberately controlled, lest he should excite anyone's attention about the barracks, and be seen carrying the Havildar's clay basin. It was with difficulty, however, that he prevented himself from stumbling, for his soul was full of love and adoration and worship for the man who had thought it fit to entrust him, an unclean menial, with the job and his eyes were turned inwards.

He went and stood in sight of a kitchen cubicle where a cook sat by the earthen fireplace peeling potatoes, while a big brass saucepan sent coils of steam shooting out from under its lid.

'Will you give me some pieces of coal for Havildar Charat Singh, please?'

The cook looked at Bakha for a moment, as much as to ask: 'Who are you?' He thought he had seen the face somewhere but he couldn't place him. 'He might be one of the sappers,' he concluded charitably, seeing that the man held Havildar Charat Singh's clay basin in his hand. As the sappers, in spite of their dark colour and dirty clothes, are of the grass-cutter caste, no one would object to sending one of them on an errand to fetch fire. Besides, the cook was indebted to Havildar Charat Singh. The Havildar had given him a clean new shirt and a white turban before he went on leave. He lifted two sticks of wood fuel from the fire and stuck them on the ground before Bakha. The sweeper picked up the live, burning pieces of coal in his hand one by one, and put them in the firepot. He suddenly recalled the figure of the little girl in his dream of the morning on whose hands the silversmith had placed a burning ember.

'*Mehrbani*' (thank you), he said, when he had half filled the firepot with coal. 'The Havildar says he wants his tea.' He tried to put a great deal of humility into an unfortunately abrupt sentence.

Then he walked back to where Charat Singh sat in an easy-chair he had drawn out from somewhere, and he handed him the firepot. The Havildar casually stretched his hand and, accepting the pot, put it on his coco-nut shell hookah and gurgled away for all he was worth.

Bakha was feeling impatient now, and he sat near the veranda on a brick. He didn't know why he felt impatient. It was because of the hookah. It always made him impatient. And then he was eager for the hockey stick. The Havildar hadn't said a word about it. 'Had he forgotten?' Bakha wondered. So as he sat waiting, he itched a bit with the empty awkwardness that yawned between him and Charat Singh. The cook came bearing a long brass tumbler and a jug of tea and the Havildar relieved his friend of his nervousness in an easy unconscious manner.

'Get that pan from which the sparrows drink water,' he said to Bakha, pointing to the foot of a wooden pillar. 'Pour out the water from it.'

Bakha did as he was directed, and the vessel was clean in his hand. To his great surprise Charat Singh got up and began to pour tea out of his tumbler into the pan.

'No, no, sir,' Bakha protested in the familiar Indian guests' manner.

Charat Singh poured out the tea.

'Drink it, drink it, my son.'

'I am very grateful, Havildar ji,' said Bakha. 'It is very kind of you.'

'Drink it, drink the tea, you work hard; it will relieve your fatigue,' said Charat Singh.

When Bakha had gulped down the liquid, he rose and replaced the vessel. Meanwhile Charat Singh had poured the contents of his jug into the tumbler and sipped it quietly.

'Now what about a hockey stick for you!' he said, licking his lips and his thin moustache with the tip of his tongue.

Bakha looked up and tried to assume a grateful expression. He didn't have to try very hard, for in, a second he seemed to have dwarfed himself to the littlest little being on earth, and followed the Havildar noiselessly. His face was hot with the tea, his teeth shone even in their slavish smile, his whole body and mind were tense with admiration and gratitude to his benefactor. 'What has happened to change my *kismet* (fate) all of a sudden?' he asked himself. 'Such kindness from the Havildar, who is a Hindu, and one of the most important men about the regiment!' He followed Charat Singh with his gaze, curiously amazed.

The Havildar opened a door by the side of his room and

disappeared for a moment. Then he came out with an almost brand-new hockey stick, which must have been used only once. He handed it to Bakha as casually as he had given him the firepot to go and fill with charcoal.

'But it is new, Havildar ji,' Bakha said as he took it.

'Now run along, new or not new, it doesn't matter,' said Charat Singh. 'Conceal it under your coat and don't tell anyone. Go, my lad.'

Bakha bent his head and evaded the Havildar's eyes. He couldn't look at so generous a person. He was overcome by the man's kindness. He was grateful, grateful, haltingly grateful, falteringly grateful, stumblingly grateful, so grateful that he didn't know how he could walk the ten yards to the corner to be out of the sight of his benevolent and generous host. The whole atmosphere was charged with embarrassment. He felt uncomfortable as he walked away. 'Strange! strange! wonderful! kind man! I didn't know he was so kind. I should have known. He always has such a humorous way about him! Kind, good man! He gave me a new stick, a brand-new stick!' He impatiently drew the stick from the folds of his overcoat where he had hidden it. It was a beautiful broad-bladed stick, marked with English stamps, and therefore, to Bakha, the best stick that had been manufactured in the world. It had a leather handle. 'Beautiful! Beautiful!' his heart seemed to be shouting in its thumping, mad rush of exhilaration. He turned the corner and went across the ditch, so that he was out of sight of his benefactor. Assured now that nobody would see the foolish pride and pleasure that he was taking in his prize, he rested it on the ground in the position in which it is usual to place a stick before hitting the ball. He bent it. It was elastic and bent finely. *That* Bakha knew was the test of a good stick. He hurriedly rubbed off the dust that had touched the lower part of the stick and holding it fast in his hands, as if he were afraid someone would come and snatch it from him, he tried to assure himself and make himself believe that he possessed it, so incredulous was he of the fact that he owned it. In spite of the fact that he held it tight, he couldn't shake off the feeling that he was dreaming, until he got to the edge of the playing-fields outside the gymnasium, behind the Indian officers' quarters, and began to hit a little round stone about. Then he suddenly realised that the stick might break, or get scarred, that way. He clutched it hard, and pressed it to his body, and tried to recollect his thoughts: 'So my normal good luck has returned. If only that thing hadn't happened this morning!'

Bakha tried to recall Charat Singh's face.

It had a slight suspicion of forgetfulness about it. 'I hope he knew what he was doing,' Bakha thought. 'I hope he wasn't absent-minded. He may have been. Dare I play with the stick? It might be spoiled, and in case he suddenly realises he has given away something he didn't want to give, it will be terrible because I can't return his stick battered or broken or even used. And, of course, I can't buy a new stick like this. But there is no question of that. Didn't he say: 'New or not new, take it and run away, and don't tell anyone.' Of course he knew what he was doing. I am mad to think that he was forgetful. So kind a person, and I think *this* about him. I am a pig to do that.' He didn't want to think at all, since he felt his thoughts becoming ungenerous. 'How beautiful the afternoon is,' he said, and he tilted his face up from the curve of, his thought to sniff the bite in the air which came from the hills in the north. He was aware of the transparent autumn sunshine, just warm enough to fill a heart wrapped in warm clothes with pleasure. The cup of Bakha's life was filled to overflowing with the happiness of the lucid, shining afternoon, as the bowl of the sky was filled with a clear and warm sunshine. He could have jumped for joy.

He was just going to, then he felt someone might see him. Someone was sure to be about. A passing sepoy or someone from among the boys. So there was no way of extending happiness into space except by walking about.

He began to walk. Each step he took was a strut, his chest thrown out, his head lifted high and his legs stiff, as if they were made of wood. The awkward sway of his rump had, for a moment, become the haughty gait of a proud soldier.

Then he caught a glimpse of himself foolishly strutting about and he grew self-conscious. He stopped suddenly, uncomfortably. His newly-assumed confidence had been shattered.

He was impatient now. He wished someone would come and relieve his loneliness. If only a sepoy were passing, he would look at him. And if one of the boys came, he would show him the stick he had acquired. He wished that Chota would come. He would like to have shown him the stick. Or Ram Charan. 'But no, I must not show it to Ram Charan. Else he will go to Charat Singh and worry him by demanding a similar stick. The Havildar said I wasn't to tell anyone. He will be angry with me if Ram Charan takes it into his head to go and beg for a stick.' He wished the babu's sons would come. They had the ball. The elder boy had promised to give him a lesson in English. Perhaps he could give it to him before the game started. He wished someone would come, someone to fill his mind, which had dried up, become suddenly empty.

He walked about aimlessly now. His limbs were loose. His face turned now to this side, now to that, with a halfconscious look. At last he espied the babu's son, the little boy, rushing out of the hall of his house, a big stick in his little hand, food in his mouth and sweets tied up in the lap of his tunic. Bakha knew how eager the little one was to play hockey. He began to advance towards the child with an easy step, made awkward by a consciousness of his low position, and with a smile of humility on his face. He liked the babu's sons, respected them, not only because they were high-caste Hindus whom he, as a sweeper's son, had to respect, but also because their father held a position of extraordinary importance in the regiment, almost second to the Colonel Sahib himself.

The little one came up to him with a wild gesture of enthusiasm and said:

'Look, here is the new stick I told you about this morning. Charat Singh gave it to me.'

'Oh, it is very beautiful!' Bakha commented. 'But,' he continued jocularly, 'look at mine, it is better than yours. Ha, ha, mine is more beautiful than yours.'

'Let me see,' said the little one.

Bakha handed him the stick.

'Oh, it is the same kind exactly!' shouted the child.

Bakha felt that Charat Singh had apparently not done him an exceptional favour. But it was a favour all right. 'The babu's sons were the babu's sons. He would, of course, give them sticks. That he had given one to him, a sweeper, was an extraordinary favour.'

'Are you prepared for the match? Ohe, Bakhe,' said the child, as if he were a full-grown skipper.

'Yes, I am ready,' said Bakha smilingly, and without betraying the slightest sign of that sympathy which he felt for the child, seeing him so enthusiastic and knowing he wouldn't be allowed to play. He liked the little one, so brimful of energy and enthusiasm.

'Where is your elder brother?' Bakha asked the child.

'He is finishing his meal. He is coming. I shall go and fetch the hockey sticks and the ball. The boys will soon be here.' And he ran home abruptly, leaving Bakha curiously affected.

'Poor little boy, and they won't let him play. He is so eager. He will be an extraordinary man when he grows up. A big babu perhaps. Or a sahib. His eyes twinkle so!—'

'Ohe, Bakhe,' someone disturbed his thoughts.

He turned round and saw Chota and Ram Charan followed by various boys, the armourer's sons, Naimat and Asmat; the tailor-master's son Ibrahim; the bandmaster's sons, Ali, Abdulla, Hassan and Hussein, and hosts of strangers, presumably the boys of the 31st Punjabis. Bakha advanced towards them. Chota ran up to him and whispered: 'I have told them that you are the sahib's bearer: they don't know that you are a sweeper.'

'All right,' Bakha agreed. He knew that it had been done to convince some of the orthodox boys of the 31st Punjabis team that they wouldn't be polluted.

'Look, I have got a wonderful new stick,' said Bakha. He showed it to his friend. Then he said: 'Don't tell Ram Charan about it. Charat Singh gave it to me. I shall score no end of goals with it.'

'Wonderful! Wonderful! Marvellous! Beautiful!' exclaimed Chota. 'Brother-in-law, you are lucky!' He slapped Bakha's back and raised a small cloud of dust from his thick overcoat.

'Boys, get ready,' he shouted as he turned.

When the time for the election of the team came, the babu's little son brought and dumped the sticks before Chota and expected his reward. But Chota had already chosen his eleven.

'Let the child play,' Bakha put in on the little one's behalf.

'No, he will be troublesome,' Chota whispered. 'We can't let him play. It is a match with the big boys. He will get hurt and then there will be trouble.'

Bakha didn't want to insist too much. He knew that Chota and the little one didn't get on very well, and he was helpless seeing he liked them both equally, hurt to see the child ignored by everyone except his elder brother, who was trying to console him by saying that even he might not be asked to play, so important was the match, and between such big boys.

The child bore the disappointment more easily when it came, after the consolation his brother had offered and the friendliness reflected in Bakha's smiles. Ignored and helpless, he sought to interest himself in the match by volunteering to be the referee. But Chota wouldn't have him even as a referee. The little one now looked sorry for himself. The match had begun. He stood by the heaps of the boys' clothes which lay on the side of the hockey ground. He wished he were as big as Chota. Then he would be asked to play. Also then he could wear shorts like him. And he would look like a real sahib because he was not so dark as Chota.

Bakha came, for a second, to throw off his overcoat near the little one. He had started playing without having discarded it.

'Keep a watch over it, little brother, won't you?' he said to the child, as if by entrusting him with the job he was trying to console him for his non-inclusion in the team. Then he ran back to his place.

The little one could have cried at that moment. But the game, the play—Bakha was going to score a goal.

It was an extraordinary spectacle. The crowd of boys in the field hopped to and fro like grasshoppers. There was no organisation in the game they played. Bakha had rolled the ball, dribbling, dodging to the goal of the 31st Punjabis boys. But then he had been caught, enmeshed, by a throng of defenders of the goal, struggling, shouting, shoving to hit the ball out. Bakha managed, however, to scoop past the legs of all the boys and drove the ball into the space between the posts.

Defeated by superior tactics, the goalkeeper spitefully struck Bakha a blow on the legs. Upon this Chota, Ram Charan, Ali, Abdulla and all the rest of the 38th Dogra boys fell upon the goalkeeper of the 31st Punjabis.

Soon there was a free fight.

'Foul! Foul!' shouted the captain of the 31st Punjabis team.

'No foul! No foul!' responded Chota, drawing himself up to his full height angrily.

The captain of the 31st Punjabis advanced hotly, tearing the hordes asunder, and gripped Chota by the collar. And, once more, the boys were fighting, scratching, hitting, kicking, yelling. One, two, three, four, five, the little hands worked their sticks, rudely, heavily, vigorously, and the blusterings of the horde reached such a pitch of excitement that you could see the ruthlessness of the savage hunters in them. Chota had gripped his antagonist by the shoulder and for a time these two wrestled furiously, wildly, tearing each other's clothes and punching each other. Then Chota's enemy, unable to endure his transgressions, called to his followers and ran back a few yards.

'Throw stones at them, stones,' shouted Chota.

At this the boys of the 38th Dogras seemed to separate from their enemies, to run on one side and to begin hurling small stones at them.

In their intense excitement they didn't notice the little boy who stood near the clothes between them and their enemies, receiving the full weight of the stone bombardment. Most of the stones, however. passed high over the child's head and, though frightened, he was safe. But a bad throw from Ram Charan's hand caught him a rap on the skull. He gave a sharp, piercing shriek and fell unconscious. All the boys rushed to him. Streams of blood were pouring from the back of his head. Bakha picked him up in his arms and took him to the hall of his house. Unfortunately for him, the child's mother had heard the row they had been making and casually came to see if her children were safe. She met Bakha face to face.

'You eater of your masters, you dirty sweeper!' she shouted. 'What have you done to my son?'

Bakha was going to open his mouth and tell her what had happened. But even while she asked, she knew from the trickling of the blood from her son's skull, from his deathly, pale, senseless face.

'Oh, you eater of your masters! What have you done? You have killed my son!' she wailed, flinging her hands across her breasts and turning blue and red with fear. 'Give him to me! Give me my child! You have defiled my house, besides wounding my son!'

'Mother, mother, what are you saying?' interposed her elder son. 'It was not he. He didn't wound him. It was the washerwoman's son Ram Charan.'

'Get away, get away, you eater of your masters!' she shouted at him. 'May you die! Why didn't you look after your brother?'

Bakha handed over the child, and afraid, humble, silent as a ghost, withdrew. He felt dejected, utterly miserable. Was the pleasure of Charat Singh's generosity only to be enjoyed for half an hour? What had he done to deserve such treatment? He loved the child. He had been very sorry when Chota refused to let him join the game. Then why should the boy's mother abuse him when he had tried to be kind? She hadn't even let him tell her how it all happened. 'Of course, I polluted the child. I couldn't help doing so. I knew my touch would pollute. But it was impossible not to pick him up. He was dazed, the poor little thing. And she abused me. I only get abuse and derision wherever I go. Pollution, pollution, I do nothing else but pollute people. They all say that: "Polluted, polluted!" She was perhaps justified though. Her son was injured. She could have said anything. It was my fault and of the other boys too. Why did we start that quarrel? It started on account of the goal I scored. Cursed me! The poor child! I hope he is not badly hurt. If only Chota had let him join the game, the little one would not have been standing where he was, and then he might have escaped getting hurt. Now where have all the boys gone?'

For the first time he became conscious that he had been walking alone. He looked around. Only the sparrows on the waste land of the sweepers' lane twittered accusingly at him in the pale afternoon light. With a sudden shudder of unutterable weariness he clutched the stick which he carried under his arm, and turned into a by-path leading to his home across decayed walnut leaves.

Before he came within sight of his home, he stopped and looked for a convenient spot where he might hide his hockey stick. He couldn't take it home. His father would at once fly into a rage about his wasting valuable time playing when there was all the work to do at the latrines. There was a long hedge of cactus away from the path. He turned towards it. There was a convenient hollow in the middle of the bush. He stepped over with a high stride into the hollow and laid the stick there. Then he bent down a few oar-shaped cactus leaves on to it and covered it against bad weather. After that he hurried, lest he should be seen hiding the stick by someone who might come later and filch it.

When Bakha returned his father sat smoking his hubble-bubble in the English wicker-chair. For a moment Lakha was unaware of his son's presence. Then suddenly he seemed to rise from his seat and wave his close-fisted hand menacingly at Bakha and to shout:

'You son of a pig! You son of a dog! You ran away! You have been away all the afternoon and now you come back! You illegally begotten! Have you become a nabob that you go wandering about when you know that there is work here for you to do? The sepoys have been shouting!'

Bakha was cool in the face of this warm reception. He was too wearied by the succession of revived memories to cope with anything now. He stood obstinately still while his father's invective continued.

'Son of a pig! You have no care for your old father. You go out in the morning and you come back at night. Who is going to do the work at the latrines? I brought you up. Won't you give me some rest in my old age? There you go trying to be a sahib when you are a sweeper's son. You illegally begotten! Dog! Pig!'

Bakha moved slowly under the rain of abuse towards the latrines. He was going to pick up a broom but he saw that his brother Rakha held it. He stopped short and looked up at his brother.

'So you have come back,' shouted Rakha self-righteously. He stared hard at his elder brother. There was the pride of the favourite in his glance.

Bakha knew that the boy was preening himself because he had put in an afternoon's work and had won his father's partiality. He didn't hate him for his overbearing manner, however. He thought of him as a child, as he really loved him. And he would have borne his impudence and his father's abuse as his due, but the boy refused to give him the broom and his father persisted in his denunciation.

'Son of a pig! illegally begotten! He has no sense of shame! *Play, play, play and wander all day.* As if he has nothing else to do!'

Bakha felt he couldn't bear the constant iteration of the same sentiments. He knew the way in which his father nagged him, persistently, stubbornly, without waiting for breath. He made for the latrines.

'Get away, you swine, run away from my presence,' shouted his father. 'Don't touch that broom or I shall kill you. Go away! Get out of my house. And don't come back! Don't let us see your face again!'

Before now, Bakha had often borne the brunt of his misery with a resigned air of fatalism. He had quietly suffered his father's abuse and satire, and even occasional beatings with a calm that betokened his intense docility and gentleness. He would never lift his head, or his hand, to defend himself against anyone. To-day, however, he had had more than enough. The spirit of fire which lay buried in the mass of his flesh had ignited this morning and lay smouldering. A little more fuel and it flared up, like a wild flame.

He tore across the plain without even looking back. It was as though a demon had taken possession of him. He was not conscious of the shattering moment which had suddenly determined his flight. Nor was he aware of the feeling of revulsion that had filled the moment. It seemed as if the demon in him held a cruel sword with which it hacked everything in its way and, by the force of the hacking, acquired a more sinister power, frightening in its intensity and weirdly fascinating in its transmutation of Bakha's body into a wild yet marvellously controlled medium.

He advanced eagerly. The old river lay on his right like a stormy sea of discontent whose mountainous waves the wind had swept, till the boulders and rocks reared up in knife-edges against the sky or rolled quietly over the earth. So different from what was on his left, the monotone of dusty plain, with short patterns of mauve and silver and grey where the sun's rays played upon the crest, and deep purple shadows in its fissures and its folds.

As he moved over the fringe of flat earth facing the plain, the rim of the upturned sky was taking on the gold and silver hues of the afternoon sun, and the world lay encircled in a ribbon of crimson. Here he slackened his pace, for it was here that he had felt the first glow of the early morning sun creeping into his bones. It was through this plain that he had gone out to the world, full of the spirit of adventure.

The wide expanse was empty except for the interminable thread of men entering the mud-houses which clustered in the north like mushrooms, surrounded by rubbish-heaps filled with broken bottles, old tins, dead cats and deep in mud. So lofty did he feel in his mood of righteous indignation that he had the strange sensation of being a giant, of commanding a full view of everything in the hollows and the hills.

'Unlucky, unlucky day! What have I done to deserve all this?' he cried in exasperation.

A sepoy on his way to the latrines was approaching. He jumped aside into a ditch so as not to be seen. He didn't want to meet anybody. He wanted to be alone and quiet, to compose himself. When the man had passed, he crept out of the ditch and made for a *pipal*-tree which stood in the plain surrounded by a clay platform. He sat down under it, facing the sun.

Now he felt desolate and the fact dawned on him that he was homeless. He had often been turned out like that. As a matter of fact when his father was angry he always threatened him and his brother with eviction. He remembered that once after his mother's death his father had locked him out all night, for not looking after the house properly. It was a winter night. The east wind blew and he was sleepy. He was tired from the day's work and yawned as he curled himself up in his overcoat behind two refuse-baskets. How he had smarted under the pain of that callousness and cruelty. Could he be the same father who, according to his own version, had gone praying to the doctor for medicine? Bakha recalled he had not spoken to his father for days after that incident. Then his grief about his unhappy position had become less violent, less rebellious. He had begun to work very hard. It had seemed to him that the punishment was good for him. For he felt he had learnt through it to put his heart into his work. He had matured. He had learnt to scrub floors, cook, fetch water besides doing his job cleaning the latrines and carting manure for sale to the fields. And in spite of the poor nourishment he got, he had developed into a big strong man, broad-shouldered, heavy-hipped, supple-armed, as near the Indian ideal of the wrestler as he wished to be.

But this present disgrace! This could do no good, he thought. It was undeserved. Why should his father object to his taking a half-holiday once in his life, especially as he knew he had been insulted in the town this morning and didn't feel like working? Then he had not spent the afternoon uselessly. He had got a new stick. But that, it occurred to him, was something which his father could not appreciate. He didn't like him to play hockey. That was what all the trouble was about, 'Rakha must have told about me,' he muttered, 'because he could not go to play. What a day I have had! Unlucky, inauspicious day! I wish I could die!' And he sat nursing his head in his hands, utterly given up to despair.

He had sat for a long while like that, his head in his hands. He felt sick and stifled with the knowledge that he was homeless and unwanted even by his own father. He had unconsciously chosen to sit down in a place where Chota or Ram Charan or someone from the outcastes' colony might recognise him. As time passed and he became conscious of the emptiness around him, he felt that the sympathy he longed for would never come.

But he was mistaken. Colonel Hutchinson, chief of the local Salvation Army, was never very far from the outcastes' colony. To his rather irreligious wife he always made the excuse that he was going out for a walk in the hills where the kingdom of Heaven was waiting to be found, though actually he went out wallowing in the mire for the sake of Jesus Christ, talking to some Untouchable among the rubbish-heaps about divinity and trinity. You couldn't miss him even if you saw him from a mile off, for he was one of the few living members of the band of Christian missionaries in India who had originated the idea that the Salvation Army ought to be dressed in the costume of the natives and live among them, if it was to achieve the true end of proselytising. And he had designed the Colonel's uniform he wore: a pair of white trousers, a scarlet jacket, a white turban with a red band across it. He had been a strong man once, if he wasn't quite the image of Eugene Sandow now. In the old days, he had plenty of hair on his head. Now, unfortunately, he was bald, his wife said, because of the infernal turban he wore, and because he was so fond of study. He also once had a turned-up moustache of the real Colonel kind, bushy and black. Now, though it was bushy, it was grey and drooped, his malicious wife said, in defeat, because she alleged that the proselytising mission of Christianity had, in his hands, been a complete failure. The number of conversions to his credit for the last twenty years being not more than five, and those five mainly from among the dirty, black Untouchables. But in justice to the Colonel's moustache, it must be said that his wife was being catty because she had a personal grievance against him. He had charmed her in his youth with his well-groomed, immaculate bearing, a conspicuous feature of which had been his fine black, upright moustache. She was a barmaid in Cambridge and had developed an aesthetic taste for the gem-like, glistening drops of wine that adorned the hair of Hutchinson's moustache when he had had a drink. She had married him for that. India, however, had embittered her. For not only did she hate the 'nigger' servants in her house, but she discovered that her husband was too studious for her gay card-playing, drinking and love-making tastes. Still, she had borne with him for a great many years, on the strength of whisky, but then Hutchinson's moustache had grown grey and it had begun to droop under the weight of age, the Colonel now being turned sixty-five. Despite all that his wife said, therefore, we must give credit to Colonel Hutchinson for his unflinching devotion to duty and loyalty to the cause which he had taken up.

He was marvellously active for his three-score years and five, laying himself in hiding as of yore in deep pits of filth or behind heaps of dung, to wait for some troubled outcaste who might be tired and hungry and would listen in his despair to the gospel of Christ. He always carried a number of copies of the Hindustani translation of the Bible under his arm, and he stuffed the pockets of his jacket and overcoat with the gospel of St. Luke, to thrust into the hands of any passer-by, be he willing or unwilling. He was a short fellow, pitiably weak and hobbling along on his stick. But the edge of his tongue was like a pair of scissors which cut the pattern of Hindustani into smithereens as a parrot snips his food into bits. The impulse that had made him think of learning Hindustani before he started his mission was a noble one considering that his work lay among the natives; the habit of muddling through the language, and never learning it properly during the thirty years of his stay in India, was most disastrous in its consequences.

'*Tum udas*' (You are sad), said the Colonel, putting his hand on Bakha's shoulder.

The sweeper-boy had the shock of his life to hear the broken Hindustani of a person he presumed to be an Englishman. He looked up with a start. He had expected that Chota or Ram Charan might come and console him, or someone from the outcastes' colony. He had not the foggiest notion that he would be surprised by Colonel Hutchinson, who although he freely mixed with the natives and had thus lost some of the glamour attaching to the superior, remote and reticent Englishmen, was yet a sahib who wore trousers and used a commode. Bakha felt honoured that the sahib had deigned to talk Hindustani to him, even though it was broken Hindustani. He felt flattered that he should be the object of pity and sympathy from a sahib. Of course, he at once recognised the Colonel. Who didn't know the missionary? But it was the first occasion on which he had found himself face to face with him. Being of a very retiring disposition and full of a feeling of inferiority he had never talked to

Hutchinson, although he remembered that the Colonel often visited his father when he (Bakha) was a child. His father, he recalled, also talked of the sahib, sometimes if he saw him in the distance, saying that the old sahib had wanted to convert them to the religion of *Yessuh Messih* and to make them sahibs like himself, but that he had refused to leave the Hindu fold, saying that the religion which was good enough for his forefathers was good enough for him.

'Salaam, Sahib,' said Bakha, putting his hand to his forehead as he got up.

'Salaam, salaam, you sit, don't disturb yourself,' squealed the Colonel in wrong, badly accented Hindustani, patting Bakha affectionately the while.

There was something wonderful in the brave effort the Colonel seemed to make to be natural in this unnatural atmosphere. But he was not self-conscious. He had thrown aside every weight—pride of birth and race and colour in adopting the customs of the natives and in garbing himself in their manner, to build up the Salvation Army in India. And he had swamped the overbearing strain of the upper middle-class Englishman in him by his hackneyed effusions of Christian sentiment, camouflaged the narrow, insular patriotism of his character in the jingo of the white-livered humanitarian.

'What has happened? Are you ill?' the Colonel asked, bending over.

Bakha felt confused, embarrassed by the flood of kindness. 'Charat Singh,' he thought, 'was kind to me this afternoon; the sahib is generosity itself.' And he wondered if he were dreaming. He looked and saw the form of the Colonel real enough before him. And hadn't he heard the strange, squeaky voice of the Englishman speaking Hindustani? good Hindustani, Bakha thought, considering it was spoken by a sahib, for ordinarily he knew the sahibs didn't speak Hindustani at all, only some useful words and swear words: '*Acha* (good); *jao* (go away); *jaidi karo* (be quick); *sur ka bacha* (son of a pig); *kute ka bacha* (son of a dog)!'

'Nothing, Sahib, I was just tired,' said Bakha shyly. 'I am sweeper here, son of Lakha, Jemadar of the sweepers.'

'I know! I know! How is your father?'

'Huzoor, he is well,' replied Bakha.

'Has your father told you who I am?' asked the Colonel, coming to the point in the practical manner of the Englishman.

'Yes, Huzoor. You are a sahib,' said Bakha.

'No, no,' pretended the Colonel. 'I am not a sahib. I am like you. I am padre of the Salvation Army.'

'Yes, Sahib, I know,' said Bakha, without understanding the subtle distinction which the Colonel was trying to institute between himself and the ordinary sahibs in India whose haughtiness and vulgarity was, to his Christian mind, shameful, and from whom, on that account, he took care to distinguish himself, lest their misdeeds reflect on the sincerity of his intentions for the welfare of the souls of the heathen. To Bakha, however, all the sahibs were sahibs, trousered and hatted men, who were generous in the extreme, giving away their cast-off clothes to their servants, also a bit nasty because they abused their servants a great deal. He knew, of course, that the Colonel was a padre sahib, but he did not know what a padre did except that he lived near the *girja ghar* (church) and came to see the people in the outcastes' colony. To him even the padres were of interest because of their European clothes. This padre did not wear a hat like the padre in the barracks of the British regiments. But that was of little account. He wore all the other items of clothes that the sahibs wore. He was a sahib all right. And this sahib had condescended to pat him on the back, to speak kind words to him, even to ask him why he was looking so sad. He could have cried to receive such gracious treatment from a sahib, cried with the joy of being in touch with that rare quality which was to be found in the sahibs. In spite of it all, however,.he seemed to be vaguely aware of the difference the Colonel was trying to define.

'I am a padre and my God is *Yessuh Messih*,' emphasised the Colonel. 'If you are in trouble, come to Jesus in the *girja ghar*.'

He was seeking vainly to paraphrase the promise: 'Come all ye that labour and I will give you rest.'

Bakha was struck with the coincidence. How did the padre know he was in trouble? 'And who is *Yessuh Messih* to whose religion my father told me this padre wanted to convert us? I wonder if he lives in the *girja ghar*?' He recalled that the *girja ghar* had seemed to him a mysterious place whenever he had passed by.

'Who is *Yessuh Messih*, Sahib?' Bakha asked, eager to allay his curiosity.

'Come, I shall tell you,' said Colonel Hutchinson. Come to the church.' And dragging the boy with his arm, babbling, babbling, all vague, in a cloud, and enthusiastic as a mystic, he led him away on the wings of a song:

'Life is found in Jesus,
Only there 'tis offered thee;
Offered without price or money
'Tis the gift of God sent free.'

Bakha was dumb with amazement, carried away by the confusion, feeling flattered, honoured by the invitation which had come from the sahib, however much that sahib looked like a native. He followed willingly, listening to each word that the Colonel spoke, but not understanding a word:

'Life is found in Jesus,'

the Colonel sang again, absorbed in himself, and unconscious that he was in charge of a soul in trouble.

Jesus! Who was Jesus! The same as *Yessuh Messih*? Who was he? The sahib says he is God. Was he a God like Rama, God of the Hindus, whom his father worshipped and his forefathers had worshipped, whom his mother used to mention quite often in her prayers? These thoughts gushed into Bakha's mind, and he would have exploded with them had it not been that the Colonel was absolutely absorbed in his sing-song:

'Life is found alone in Jesus,
Only there 'tis offered thee;
Offered without price or money;
'Tis the gift of God sent free.'

'Huzoor,' said Bakha, breaking in impatiently at the close of
the third recitation,' who is Jesus? The same as *Yessuh Messih*?
Who is he?'

'He died that we might be forgiven,
He died to make us good,
That we might go at last to heaven,
Saved by His precious blood,'

answered the Colonel quickly, rhythmically, before Bakha knew
what he had asked. He was still baffled. The answer, if it was
an answer, was like a conundrum to him; words, words. He felt
overwhelmed and uncomfortable. But being, of course, too happy
to be seen walking with the sahib, he bore all, trying to
remember parts of the Colonel's song and asking himself what
they meant. But apart from the muffled sound of words he could
not catch anything.

'Sahib, who is *Yessuh Messih*?'

'He is the Son of God,' answered Colonel Hutchinson,
coming down to earth for a moment. 'He died that we might be
forgiven.'

And then he burst into song again:
He died that we might be forgiven,
He died to make us good,
That we might go at last to heaven,
Saved by His precious blood.'

'He died that we might be forgiven,' thought Bakha. 'What
does that mean? He is the son of God! How could anybody be
the son of God if God, as my mother told me, lives in the sky?
How could He have a son? And why did His son die that we

117

should be forgiven? Forgiven for what? And who is this son of God?'

'Who is *Yessuh Messih*, Sahib? Is he the God of the sahibs?' Bakha asked, slightly afraid that he was bothering the white man too much. He knew from experience that Englishmen did not like to talk too much.

'He is the Son of God, my boy,' answered the Colonel, ecstatically revolving his head. 'And He died for us sinners:

He died that we might be forgiven,
He died to make us good,
That we might go at last to heaven,
Saved by His precious blood.'

Bakha was a bit bored by this ecstatic hymn-singing. But the white man had condescended to speak to him, to take notice of him. He was happy and proud to be in touch with a sahib. He suffered the priest and even reiterated his enquiry:

'Do they pray to *Yessuh Messih* in your *girja ghar*, Sahib?'

'Yes, yes,' replied the Colonel, breaking into the rhythm of a new hymn:

Jesus, tender shepherd, hear me.
Let my sins be forgiven!
Let there be light,
Oh, shed Thy light in the heart of this boy.'

Bakha was baffled and bored. He did not understand anything of these songs. He had followed the sahib because the sahib wore trousers. Trousers had been the dream of his life. The kindly interest which the trousered man had shown him when he was downcast had made Bakha conjure up pictures of himself wearing the sahib's clothes, talking the sahib's language and becoming like the guard whom he had seen on the railway station near his village. He did not know who *Yessuh Messih* was. The sahib probably wanted to convert him to his religion. He didn't want to be converted. But he wouldn't mind being converted if he knew who *Yessuh Messih* was. The sahib, however, was singing, singing to himself and saying *Yessuh Messih* was the son of God. How could God have a son? Who is God? If God is like Rama, He has no son, for he had never heard that Rama had a son. It was all so puzzling that he thought of excusing himself by lying to the sahib that he had to go to work and couldn't come with him. The Colonel saw Bakha lagging behind and, realising that his new follower was losing interest, exerted the peculiar obstinacy of the enthusiastic missionary in him and dragging at the boy's sleeve, said, '*Yessuh Messih* is the Son of God, my boy. While we were yet sinners, He died for us. He sacrificed Himself for us.' Then again he became rapt in his devotional songs:

'O Calvary! O Calvary!
It was for me that Jesus died
On the Cross of Calvary!'

He sacrificed himself for us, Bakha reflected. His idea of sacrifice was something very certain and definite. He remembered that when some calamity brooded over the family, such as an epidemic of sickness, or starvation, his mother used to make offerings to the goddess Kali, by sacrificing a goat or some other animal. That sacrifice was supposed to appease the goddess's wrath and the evil passed over. Now, what did this sacrifice of *Yessuh Messih* mean? Why did he sacrifice himself?

'Why did *Yessuh Messih* sacrifice himself, Huzoor?' he asked.

'He died that we might be forgiven,
He died to make us good,
That we might go at last to heaven,
Saved by His precious blood,'

answered the Colonel, forgetting, as he had often done while he had been with Bakha, that the sweeper-boy didn't understand a word of what he was singing. Then in a sane moment he recognised the look of anxious solicitude on the face of the boy and realised he had been babbling too much, and mostly to himself.

'He sacrificed Himself out of love for us,' he said. 'He sacrificed Himself to help us all; for the rich and the poor for Brahmin and the Bhangi.' The last sentence went home. 'He sacrificed himself for us, for the rich and the poor, for the 'Brahmin and the Bhangi.' That meant there was no difference in his eyes between the rich and the poor, between the Brahmins and the Bhangis, between the pundit of the morning, for instance, and himself.

'Yes, yes, Sahib, I understand,' said Bakha eagerly. '*Yessuh Messih* makes no difference between the Brahmin and myself.'

'Yes, yes, my boy, we are all alike in the eyes of Jesus,' the Colonel answered him. But he began garrulously: 'He is our superior. He is the Son of God. We are all sinners. He will intercede with God, His Father, on our behalf.'

'He is superior to us. We are all sinners. Why, why is anyone superior to another? Why are we all sinners? Bakha began to reflect.

'Why are we all sinners, Sahib?' he queried.

'We were all born sinners,' replied the Colonel evasively, the puritan in him shying at an exposition of the doctrine of original sin which seemed called for.

'We must confess our sins. Then alone will He forgive us, otherwise we will have to suffer the eternal torment of hell. You confess your sins to me before I convert you to Christianity.

'But, Huzoor, I don't know who *Yessuh Messih* is. I know Ram. But I don't know *Yessuh Messih*.'

'Ram is the god of the idolaters,' the Colonel said after a pause, and a bit absent-mindedly. 'Come and confess your sins to me and *Yessuh Messih* will receive you in Heaven when you die.'

Now Bakha was utterly bored. Never mind if it was a sahib who was giving him his company. He was afraid of the thought of conversion. He hadn't understood very much of what the

Salvationist said. He didn't like the idea of being called a sinner. He had committed no sin that he could remember. How could he confess his sins? Odd. What did it mean, confessing sins? 'Does the sahib want some secret knowledge?' he wondered. 'Does he want to perform some magic or get some illegal knowledge?' He didn't want to go to Heaven. As a Hindu he didn't believe in the judgment day. He had never thought of that. He had seen people die. And he just accepted the fact. He had been told that people who died were reborn in some form or other. He dreaded that he should be reborn as a donkey or a dog. But all that didn't disturb him. '*Yessuh Messih* must be a good man,' he thought, 'if he regards a Brahmin and a Bhangi the same.' But who was he? Where did he come from? What did he do? He had heard the story of Ram. He had heard the story of Krishna. But he hadn't heard the story of *Yessuh Messih*. 'This sahib will not tell me the story,' he said to himself. But he still hoped he might give him a pair of his cast-off trousers. And he followed him half unwillingly.

'Look, that is our home,' said the Colonel, reaching the gate of a compound leading to a pile of mud-houses among the neem-trees with thatched and sloping roofs.

'I know, Sahib,' said Bakha, who had often passed by it.

'It was a drug-house once, an opium distillery,' said the Colonel with great pride. 'But five years ago we took it.' He paused for a moment to recall the trouble it had cost him to acquire the piece of land to erect a building, and he burst out piously into an exclamation of his gratitude to Christ. 'O Lord, how great are Thy works, and Thy thoughts how deep! God has indeed brought light into the world!' Then turning from his thoughts to the young man, he said: 'He has cast out the heathen from the place.'

A muffled song proceeded from the tall mud-house in the centre of the compound, which Bakha knew to be the *girja ghar*. The Colonel gave it shape for the benefit of the young man by lifting his finger and reciting:

'Share your blessings, share your blessings,
Share them day by day;
Share your blessings, all life's long way;
Share your blessings, though you've only one,
And it will surprise you how much good you've done.'

'George, George, tea is ready!' came a shrieking, hoarse and hysterical voice, tearing the Colonel's squeaky song to bits.

'Coming, coming!' responded the Colonel automatically, standing where he stood, but with his arms and legs all in a flurry. He had heard his wife's voice. He was afraid of her. He was confused. He didn't know whether to go into the mud-house on the right which was his bungalow, and to take Bakha in there, or to take him to the church. He stood hesitating on the edge of a conflict.

'Where are you? Where have you been all the afternoon?' came the shrieking voice again. And behind it appeared the form of a round-faced, big-bellied, dark-haired, undersized, middle-aged woman, a, long cigarette-holder with a cigarette in her mouth, a gaily-coloured band on her Eton-cropped hair, pince-nez glasses on her rather small eyes, a low-necked printed cotton frock that matched her painted and powdered face and reached barely down to her knees.

'Oh, is that what you've been doing, going to these blackies again!' she shouted, frowning, her heavily-powdered face showing its layers of real, vivid scarlet skin underneath the coating. 'I give you up. Really you're incorrigible. I should have thought you would have learned your lesson from the way those Congress wallahs beat you last week!'

'What is the matter? I am just coming. I am coming,' responded the Colonel, impatient, disturbed and embarrassed.

Bakha was going to slip away in order to save the Colonel the displeasure of his wife, for which, he felt, he was mainly responsible.

'Wait, wait,' said the Colonel, holding the sweeper-boy's hand. 'I'll take you to the church.'

122

'So that the tea should get cold!' exclaimed Mary Hutchinson. 'I can't keep waiting for you all day while you go messing about with all those dirty *bhangis* and *chamars*,' and saying this, she withdrew into her boudoir.

Bakha had not known the exact reason for her frowns, but when he heard the words *bhangi* and *chamar* he at once associated her anger with the sight of himself.

'Salaam, Sahib,' he said, extricating his hand from the old man's grasp before the missionary realised he had done so. And he showed his heels; such was his fear of the woman.

'Wait, wait, my son, wait,' cried the padre after him.

But in the white haze of the afternoon sun he hurried away as if the Colonel's wife were a witch, with raised arms and crooked feet following him, harassing him.

The old man was piously reciting another hymn as he stood staring at Bakha's receding figure:

'Blessed by Thy love, blessed be Thy name.'

'Everyone thinks us at fault,' Bakha was saying to himself as he walked along. 'He wants me to come and confess my sins. And his mem-sahib! I don't know what she said about *bhangis* and *chamars*. She was angry with the sahib. I am sure I am the cause of the mem-sahib's anger. I didn't ask the padre to come and talk to me. He came of his own accord. I was so happy to talk to him. I would certainly have asked him for a pair of white trousers had the mem-sahib not been angry.'

He walked along, vacantly oppressed by the weight of his heavy cloud of memories. He felt a kind of nausea in his stomach—the spiritual nausea that seemed to rise in him when he was in difficulties. He was unnerved again as in the morning after his unfortunate experiences. Only, he was now too tired to care. He just let himself be carried by his legs towards the edge of the day. There was a faint smell of wetness oozing from the dusty earth which paved his way, a sort of moist warmth that rose to his nostrils. High above the far-distant horizon of the Bulashah dales the sun stood fixed, motionless and undissolved, as if it could not bring itself to go, to move or to melt. In the hills and fields, however, there was a strange quickening. Long rows of birds flew over against the cold blue sky towards their homes. The grasshoppers chirped in an anxious chorus as they fell back into the places where they always lay waiting for food. A lone beetle sent electric waves of sound quivering into the cool clear air. Every blade of grass along the pathway, where Bakha walked, was gilded by the light.

As he went on, striding lightly from his heavy rumps, his head bent, his eyes half closed, his lower lip pressed forward, he felt the blood coursing through his veins. He seemed full of a sort of tired restlessness. The awkwardness of the moment when the missionary's wife emerged from her room on to the veranda of her thatched bungalow and glared at her husband, stirred in his soul the echoes of those memories which had shaken and stirred him during the morning. There was a common quality in the look of hate in the round white face of the Colonel's wife and in the sunken visage of the touched man. The man's protruding lower jaw, with its transparent muscles, shaken in his spluttering speech, came before Bakha's eyes. Also his eyes emerging out of their sockets. The Colonel's wife had also opened her little eyes like that, behind her spectacles. That had frightened Bakha, frightened him much-more than the thrust of the touched man's eyeballs, for she was a mem-sahib, and the frown of a mem-sahib had the strange quality of unknown, uncharted seas of anger behind it. To Bakha, therefore, the few words which she had uttered carried a dread a hundred times more terrible than the fear inspired by the whole tirade of abuse by the touched man. It was probably that the episode of the morning was a matter of history, removed in time and space from the more recent scene, also, perhaps, because the anger of a white person mattered more. The mem-sahib was more important to his slavish mind than the man who was touched, he being one of his many brown countrymen. To displease the mem-sahib was to him a crime for which no punishment was bad enough. And he thought he had got off comparatively lightly. He dared not think unkind thoughts about her. So he unconsciously transferred his protest against her anger to the sum of his reactions against the insulting personages of the morning.

His attention was diverted to a black leper who sat swathed in tattered garments, exposing his raw wounds to the sun and the flies by the wayside, his crumpled hand lifted in beggary, and on his lips the prayer: '*Baba pesa de*' (Oh, man, give me a pice). Bakha had a sudden revulsion of feeling. He looked away from the man. It was the Grand Trunk Road near the railway station of Bulashah. The pavements were crowded with beggars. A woman wailed for food outside one of the many cook-shops which lined one side of the road. She had a little child in her arms, another child in a bag on her back, a third holding on to her skirt. Some boys were running behind the stream of carriages begging for coppers. Bakha felt a queer sadistic delight staring at the beggars moaning for alms but not receiving any. They seemed to him despicable. And the noise they made through their wailings and moanings and blessings oppressed him.

He heard the rumbling thunder of a railway train which passed under the footbridge he was ascending. Almost simultaneously he heard a shout from the golbagh garden rend the still, leafy air. The shadow of the smoke-cloud that the engine had sent up to the bridge choked Bakha's throat and blinded his eyes. Then the fumes of smoke melted like invisible, intangible flakes of snow, leaving a dark trail of soot behind. This too paled in the sunshine. The train had rushed into the cool darkness of the tin roof on Bulashah station.

Two choruses of voices tore through the air this time one charged the sky from the platform where the train had stopped; another rose above the tree-tops of the golbagh, undulating from horizon to horizon.

Bakha stood for a moment on the platform of the footbridge

and stared towards the tin roof. Myriads of faces were jutting out of white clothes. He looked in the direction of the golbagh. A veritable sea of white tunics faced him in the oval, where, ordinarily, he had seen the city gymkhana play cricket. Now there was a profound silence. He waited in the hush and listened. The chorus began again. As a spark of lightning suddenly inumines the sky, the myriad of voices leapt up the curve of the heavens before Bakha and wrote in flaming colours the cry: '*Mahatma Gandhi ki-jai*.' And, in a while, there was a rush of eager feet ascending the footbridge behind him shouting: 'The Mahatma has come! The Mahatma has come!'

Before Bakha had turned round to look at them, they were descending the steps south of the bridge. A passing man answered the questioning look of all the pedestrians by informing them that there was going to be a meeting in the golbagh, where the Mahatma was going to speak.

At once the crowd, and Bakha among them, rushed towards the golbagh. He had not asked himself where he was going. He hadn't paused to think. The word 'Mahatma' was like a magical magnet to which he, like all the other people about him, rushed blindly. The wooden boards of the footbridge creaked under the eager downward rush of his ammunition boots. He began to take several steps at a stride. He was so much in a hurry that he didn't even remember the fact of his being an Untouchable, and actually touched a few people. But not having his broom and basket with him, and the people being all in a flurry, no one noticed that a sweeper-boy had brushed past him. They hurried by.

At the foot of the bridge, by the tonga and motor-lorry stand, the road leading to the fort past the entrance of the golbagh looked like a regular racecourse. Men, women and children of all the different races, colours, castes and creeds, were running towards the oval. There were Hindu lallas from the piece-goods market of Bulashah, smartly dressed in silks; there were Kashmiri Muhammadans from the local carpet factories, immaculately clad in white cotton; there were the rough Sikh rustics from the near-by villages swathed in handspun cloth, staves in their hands and loads of shopping on their backs; there were fierce-looking red cheeked Pathans shirted in red stuff, followers of Abdul Gaffar Khan, the frontier revolutionary; there were the black-faced Indian Christian girls from the Salvation Army colony, in short coloured skirts, blouses and aprons; there were people from the outcastes' colony, whom Bakha recognised in the distance, but whom he was too rushed to greet; there was here and there a stray European—there was everybody going to meet the Mahatma, to pay homage to Mohandas Karam Chand Gandhi. And like Bakha they hadn't stopped to ask themselves why they were going. They were just going; the act of going, of walking, running, hurrying, occupied them. Their present motive was to get there, to get there somehow, as quickly as possible. Bakha wished, as he sped along, that there were a sloping bridge on which he could have rolled down to the oval.

He saw that the fort road was too long and too congested. Suddenly, like a stag at bay, he swerved round to a little marsh made by the overflow of a municipal pipe in a corner of the golbagh, jumped the fence into the garden, much to the consternation of the sweet-peas and the pansies which grew on the edges, but wholly to the satisfaction of the crowd behind him, which, once it had got the lead, followed like sheep. The beautiful garden bowers planted by the ancient Hindu kings and since then neglected were thoroughly damaged as the mob followed behind Bakha. It was as if the crowd had determined to crush everything, however ancient or beautiful, that lay in the way of their achievement of all that Gandhi stood for. It was as if they knew, by an instinct surer than that of conscious knowledge, that the things of the old civilisation must be destroyed in order to make room for those of the new. It seemed as if, in trampling on the blades of green grass, they were deliberately, brutally trampling on a part of themselves which they had begun to abhor, and from which they wanted to escape to Gandhi.

Beyond the bowers, on the oval, was a tumult, and the throng of the thousands who had come to worship. The eager babble of the crowd, the excited gestures, the flow of emotion, portended one thought and one thought alone in the surging crowd—Gandhi. There was a terror in this devotion, half expressed, half suppressed, of the panting swarms that pressed round. Bakha stopped short as he reached the pavilion end of the cricket ground. He leant by a tree. He wanted to be detached. It wasn't that he had lost grip of the emotion that had brought him swirling on the tide of the rushing stream of people. But he became aware of the fact of being a sweeper by the contrast which his dirty khaki uniform presented to the white garments of most of the crowd. There was an insuperable barrier between himself and the crowd, the barrier of caste. He was part of a consciousness which he could share and yet not understand. He had been lifted from the gutter, through the barriers of space, to partake of a life which was his, and yet not his. He was in the midst of a humanity which included him in its folds and yet debarred him from entering into a sentient, living, quivering contact with it. Gandhi alone united him with them, in the mind, cause Gandhi was in everybody's mind, including Bakha's. Gandhi might unite them really. Bakha waited for Gandhi.

Eager and unconscious, he recalled all that he had heard of this man. People said he was a saint, that he was an *avatar* (incarnation) of the gods Vishnu and Krishna. Only recently he had heard that a spider had woven a web in the house of the *Lat Sahib* (Viceroy) at *Dilli* (Delhi), making a portrait of the sage, and writing his name under it in English. That was said to be a warning to the sahibs to depart from Hindustan, since God Almighty Himself had sent a message to a little insect that Gandhi was to be the Maharajaha of the whole of Hindustan. That the spider's web appeared in the *Lat Sahib's kothi* (Viceroy's residence) was surely significant. And they said that no sword could cut his body, no bullet could pierce his skin, no fire could scorch him!

'The *Sarkar* (Govemmeni) is afraid of him,' said a lalla standing by Bakha. 'The magistrate has withdrawn his order against Gandhiji's entry into Bulashah.'

'That is nothing, they have released him unconditionally from gaol,' chimed in a babu, spitting out a phrase of the *Tribune*, pompously, in order to show off his erudition.

'Will he really overthrow the government?' asked a rustic.

'He has the *shakti* (power) to change the whole world,' replied the babu, and he began to vomit out the whole article about Gandhi that he had crammed from the *Tribune* that morning. 'This British Govemment is nothing. Every country in Europe and America is passing through terrible convulsions, politically, economically and industrially. The people of *Vilayat* (England), the *Angrez log* (the English), are less convulsed on account of their innate conservatism, but very soon every country on earth including *Vilayat* will be faced with problems that cannot be solved without a fundamental change in the mental and moral outlook of the West. Without a radical change from a hankering after sense-gratification, which is the goal of Western civilisation, through a striving after sense-control, whether in individual or in group life, which is the essence of India's *dharmic* (religious) culture! India has been the privileged home of the world's eternal religion, that teaches how every man and woman, according to their birth and environment, must practise *swadharma* (sense-control), how through sense control they must evolve their higher nature, and so realise the bliss of divinity, deep-seated in the hearts of all beings. For this bliss all humanity blindly pants, not knowing that neither cigarettes nor cinemas nor sense-enjoyment can lead to the path of *dharmic* discipline, which alone is the highest bliss to be realised . . . Gandhi will reveal this path to the modern world, he will teach us the true religion of God-love which is the best *swaraj* (self-government). . .'

'How clever you are, Babu,' said the peasant, staring at the lecturer. He was impressed by the babu's speech, but baffled. To him Gandhi was a legend, a tradition, an oracle. He had heard from time to time during the last fourteen years how a saint had arisen as great as Guru Nanak, the incarnation of Krishna-ji-Maharaj, of whom the *Ferungi Sarkar* (English Government) was very afraid. His wife had told him of the miracles which this saint was performing. It was said that he slept in a temple one night with his feet towards the shrine of the god. When the Brahmins had chastised him for deliberately turning his feet towards God, he told them that God was everywhere and asked them to turn his feet in the direction where God was not. Upon this the priests turned his feet in the direction opposite to the one where the image of the god was, and lo the shrine of God moved in the direction of his feet. He had hungered for a sight of the saint since then. His wife wouldn't be content with anything less than a touch of the Holy Man's feet. But it was a good thing she wasn't with him. The peasant reflected that if she had come, the boys would have wished to accompany her, and they might have been crushed to death in the throng. It was a good thing they didn't know. For myself, I am glad I shall see him. It is lucky he is coming on the day that I came out shopping.

Bakha had listened hard to the babu, and, although he couldn't follow every sentence of his rhetorical outburst, he had somehow got the sense of it all.

'Tell me, Babu,' Bakha heard the yokel say to the round, felt-capped, bespectacled man who had made the oration, 'will he look after the canals when the *Ferungis* (British) have gone?' It seemed the peasant had more than a vague idea of what Gandhi was about.

'*Bhai ji* (brother), don't you know,' said the babu, 'that according to Mr. Radha Kumud Muker ji we had canals in ancient India four thousand years before Christ? Who made the Grand Trunk Road? Not the British!'

'But what about the *mukadamas* (lawsuits)?' asked the jat rustic. 'The five elders of my village use the *Panchayat* (committee of five) to wreak vengeance on their enemies, or to bring pressure on the village menials, if they become too independent, and I hear Gandhi says we must not go to the *Sarkari Adalat* (British Courts of Justice), but must take up our suits to the *Panchayat*.'

'A good *Panchayat*,' replied the babu sonorously, 'can get the villagers to do their bit from time to time in preventing damage by erosion and other causes. It may not be a good judicial body now, but it was, and always has been so in the past. So far as affairs of executive action are concerned, however, you know that the *Panchayats* have done much good in the service of this country, in the cause of good administration in general, in making walls, rebuilding roads, etc.'

The peasant didn't understand that. Nor did Bakha. But the mention of village menials by the peasant recalled to Bakha's mind the fact that he had heard that Gandhi was very keen on uplifting the Untouchables. Hadn't it been rumoured in the outcastes' colony, lately, that Gandhi was fasting for the sake of the *bhangis* and *chamars*? Bakha could not quite understand what fasting had to do with helping the low-castes. 'Probably he thinks we are poor and can't get food,' he vaguely surmised, 'so he tries to show that even he doesn't have food for days.'

'We are willing to do all we can,' the lalla disturbed Bakha's cogitations with a dramatic gesture towards the babu. 'We can boycott Manchester cotton and Bradford fancies, if it is going to mean that in the end we will have a monopoly of *swadeshi* cloth. I hear, however, that Gandhi ji is making terms with Japan.'

'You must ask the Mahatma that,' the babu replied, flurried because he heard noises at the gate from which he presumed that Gandhi was approaching. He wanted to work his way to a position from which he could obtain a good view of the great man.

'Mahatma ji is not speaking about *swadeshi*, or on civil disobedience,' put in a Congress volunteer authoritatively. 'The government has allowed him out of gaol only if he will keep strictly within the limits of his propaganda for *harijans* (men of God, as Gandhi chooses to call the Untouchables), for the removal of untouchability.' And he walked away after this declamation, showing a little of the glory that he assumed, on account of his powerful position, as an official appointed to serve the community, during the reception to be given to Gandhi.

'*Harijan!*' Bakha wondered what that meant. He had heard the word before in connection with Gandhi. 'But it has something to do with us, the *bhangis* and *chamars*,' he said to himself. 'We are *harijans*.' He recalled how some Congress men had come to the outcastes' street a month ago and lectured about *harijans*, saying they were no different from the Hindus and their touch did not mean pollution. The phrase, as it dropped from the mouth of the volunteer, had gone through Bakha's soul and body. He knew it applied to him. 'It is good that I came!' he thought. 'Is he really going to talk about the outcastes, about us, about Chota, Ram Charan, my father and me? What will he say, I wonder? Strange that the sahib of the *Mukti* (Salvation Army) said that the rich and the poor, the Brahmins and *bhangis*, are the same. Now Gandhi Mahatma will talk about us! It is good that I came. If only he knew what had happened to me this morning. I would like to get up and tell him.' He imagined himself rising on the platform, when all was still and the meeting had begun, and telling the Mahatma that a man from the city, where he had come to remove untouchability, had abused him for accidentally touching him and had also beaten him. Then the Mahatma would chastise that man perhaps, or, at least, he would chide the citizens here, and they won't treat me again as they did this morning. He seemed to get a thrill imagining himself in this scene. He felt theatrical. Then a queer stirring started in his stomach. He was confused. His face was flushed and his ears reddened. His breath came and went quickly. A chorus of '*Mahatma Gandhi ki-ji*' released his tension, as it came from the distance and chilled the heat of his body with a sudden fear that it brought into his soul.

He looked across and saw that a vast crowd had rushed the gates of the golbagh and surrounded a motor-car in which, presumably, the Mahatma was travelling. He didn't know what to do, stand still or rush. He realised he couldn't rush even though the Mahatma had abolished all caste distinctions for the day. He might touch someone and then there would be a scene. The Mahatma would be too far away to come and help him. He hesitated for a moment, then he looked at the tree overhead. There were some people perched on the branches like eagles waiting for their prey. He made for the trunk. His ammunition boots were an encumbrance but he scrambled up; using his knees as rests against the round trunk. He looked not unlike an ape as he sat commanding a view of the advancing procession along the road.

Behind a screen of flower petals showered by ardent devotees under many-coloured flags, with garlands of marigolds, jasmine and molseri around his neck, amid cries of 'Mahatma Gandhi ki-jai. Hindu—Mussulman—Sikh ki-jai, Harijan ki-jai,' the great little man came into sight. His body was swathed in a milk-white blanket, and only his dark clean-shaven head was visible, with its protruding big ears, its expansive forehead, its long nose, bridged by a pair of glasses which were divided in the lenses in two, the upper for looking, the lower for reading. There was a quixotic smile on his thin lips, something Mephistophelean in the determined little chin immediately under his mouth and the long toothless jaws resting on his small neck. But withal there was something beautiful and saintly in the face, whether it was the well-oiled scalp that glistened round the little tuft of hair on the top, or the aura of the astral self that shone like an aureole about him.

Bakha looked at the Mahatma with a mixed feeling of wonder and fear. The sage seemed to him like a child as he sat huddled up between two women, an Indian and an Englishwoman.

'That's Mrs. Kasturabai Gandhi,' Bakha heard a schoolboy whisper to a friend who sat on a branch of the tree next to him.

'And who is the other lady?' the boy asked.

'Mahatma ji's English disciple, Miss Slade, Miraben. She is the daughter of an English Admiral.'

'He is black like me,' Bakha said to himself. 'But, of course, he must be very educated.' And he waited tensely for the car which was marooned right under his eyes among the throngs of men and women seeking to touch the Mahatma's feet. The Congress volunteers struggled to carve a way through the turbans and fezes and boat-like Gandhi caps, and at last they succeeded in getting the car under way. Half pushed, half towed with the engines shut off, the chauffeur steered the vehicle to the gate, improvised at one end of the oval, with broad-leafed banana-trees decorated with flowers and paper-chains.

Bakha saw a sallow-faced Englishman, whom, he knew to be the District Superintendent of Police, standing by the roadside in a khaki uniform of breeches, polished leather gaiters and blue-puggareed, khaki sun helmet, not as smart as the military officers', but, of course, possessing for Bakha all the qualities of the sahibs' clothes. Somehow, however, at this moment Bakha was not interested in sahibs, probably because in the midst of this enormous crowd of Indians, fired with an enthusiasm for their leader, the foreigner seemed out of place, insignificant, the representative of an order which seemed to have nothing to do with the natives.

'Mahatma Gandhi ki-jai, Mahatma Gandhi ki-jai,' the cry went thundering up into the smoke-scented evening. Even Bakha's attention was switched off the man who held the sceptre of British rule in the form of his formidable truncheon, and turned to the diminutive figure of the Mahatma, now seated in the lotus seat on the Congress *pandal* (platform), surrounded by devotees, who had come soft-footed up the steps, joined hands in obeisance to the master, touched the dust at his feet, and scattered to sit around him.

The Mahatma raised his right arm from the folds of his shawl and blessed the crowd with a gentle benediction. The babble of voices died out, as if he had sent an electric shock through the mass of humanity gathered at his feet. This strange man seemed to have the genius that could, by a single dramatic act, rally multicoloured, multi-tongued India to himself. Someone stood up to chant a hymn. The Mahatma had closed his eyes and was praying. In the stillness of the moment Bakha forgot all the details of his experience during the day, the touched man, the priest, the woman in the alley, his father, Chota, Ram Charan, the walk in the hills, the missionary and his wife. Except for the turbaned, capped and aproned heads of the men and women sitting on the grass before him, his eyes seemed intent on one thing and one thing alone, Gandhi, and he heard each syllable of the Hindu hymn:

'The dawn is here, O traveller, arise;
Past is the night, and yet sleep seals thine eyes.
Lost is the soul that sleeps—dost not thou know?
The sleepless one finds peace beyond all woe.

Oh, waken! Shed thou off thy slumber deep,
Remember him who made thee and oh, weep.
For shame, is this the way of love—to sleep
When he himself doth ceaseless vigil keep?

Repent, O soul, from sin and find release,
O erring one, in sin there is no peace.
What boots it now to mourn on bended knees,
When thou thyself didst thine own load increase?

What thou wouldst do to-morrow do to-day,
Do thou the task that thou must face to-day.
What shall avail thy sorrow and dismay
When thieving birds have borne thy grain away?'

Then his attention began to flag. His mind wandered. He thought of the race he had to run to get here. He noticed how still everyone was. It irked him to see everyone so serious. The silence was getting on his nerves. But a part of him seemed to have flown, to have evaporated. He felt he had lost something of himself and was uneasy on account of it, yet thrilled about it, happy. He felt pleased to be sharing the privilege of being in a crowd gathered before the Mahatma. The hymn seemed so heavy. Yet the other feeling was light. The sage seemed so pure. Yet there was something intimate and warm about him. He smiled like a child. Bakha gazed at him. It was the only way in which he could escape feeling self-conscious. By doing that he forgot himself and everything else, as he felt he ought. The brown and black faces below him were full of a stilled rapture. He sought to feel like them, attentively absorbed. Luckily for him, just then, the Mahatma began his speech. It was a faint whisper at first, the Mahatma's voice, as it came through a loud-speaker:

'I have emerged,' he said slowly, as if he were measuring each word and talking more to himself than to anyone else, 'from the ordeal of a penance, undertaken for a cause which is as dear to me as life itself. The British Government sought to pursue a policy of divide and rule in giving to our brethren of the depressed classes separate electorates in the Councils that will be created under the new constitution. I do not believe that the bureaucracy is sincere in its efforts to elaborate the new constitution. But it is one of the conditions under which I have been released from gaol that I shall not carry on any propaganda against the government. So I shall not refer to that matter. I shall only speak about the so-called "Untouchables," whom the government tried to alienate from Hinduism by giving them a separate legal and political status.

'As you all know, while we are asking for freedom from the grip of a foreign nation, we have ourselves, for centuries, trampled underfoot millions of human beings without feeling the slightest remorse for our iniquity. For me the question of these people is moral and religious. When I undertook to fast unto death for their sake, it was in obedience to the call of my conscience.'

Bakha didn't understand these words. He was restless. He hoped the Mahatma wouldn't go on speaking of things he (Bakha) couldn't understand. He found his wish fulfilled, for a potent word interpreted his thoughts.

'I regard untouchability,' the Mahatma was saying, 'as the greatest blot on Hinduism. This view of mine dates back to the time when I was a child.'

That was getting interesting. Bakha pricked up his ears. 'I was hardly yet twelve when this idea dawned on me. A scavenger named Uka, an Untouchable, used to attend our house for cleaning the latrines. Often I would ask my mother why it was wrong to touch him, and why I was forbidden to do so. If I accidentally touched Uka I was asked to perform ablutions; and though I naturally obeyed, it was not without smilingly protesting that untouchability was not sanctioned by religion and that it was impossible that it should be so. I was a very dutiful and obedient child; but, so far as was consistent with respect for my parents, I often had tussles with them on this matter. I told my mother that she was entirely wrong in considering physical contact with Uka as sinful; it could not be sinful.

'While on my way to school, I used to touch the Untouchables; and, as I never would conceal the fact from my parents, my mother would tell me that the shortest cut to purification after the unholy touch, was to cancel it by touching a Mussulman passing by. Therefore, simply out of reverence and regard for my mother, I often did so, but never did it believing it to be a religious obligation.'

As each part of the story which the Mahatma related about the beginning of his interest in untouchability fell on his ear, Bakha felt as if he were Uka, the scavenger. By feeling like that, he thought, he would be nearer the sage, who seemed a real and genuine sympathiser. 'But the speech, the speech,' he became aware that he was missing the words of the Mahatma's speech. He eagerly returned to attention and caught the narrative at:

'The fact that we address God as "the purifier of the polluted souls" makes it a sin to regard anyone born in Hinduism as polluted—it is satanic to do so. I have never been tired of repeating that it is a great sin. I do not say that this thing crystallised in me at the age of twelve, but I do say that I did then regard untouchability as a sin.

'I was at Nellore on the National Day. I met the Untouchables there, and I prayed as I have done to-day. I do want to attain spiritual deliverance. I do not want to be reborn. But if I have to be reborn, I should wish to be reborn as an Untouchable, so that I may share their sorrows, sufferings and the affronts levelled at them, in order that I may endeavour to free myself and them from their miserable condition. Therefore I prayed that, if I should be born again, I should be so, not as a *Brahmin*, *Kshatriya*, *Vaishya*, *Shudra*, but as an outcaste, as an Untouchable.

'I love scavenging. In my ashram an eighteen-year-old Brahmin lad is doing a scavenger's work, in order to teach the *ashram* scavenger cleanliness. The lad is no reformer. He was born and bred in orthodoxy. He is a regular reader of the *Gita*, and faithfully says his prayers. When he conducts the prayers, his soft melodies melt one in love. But he felt that his accomplishments were incomplete until he had also become a perfect sweeper. He felt that if he wanted the *ashram* sweeper to do his work well he must do it himself and set an example.'

Bakha felt thrilled to the very marrow of his bones. That the Mahatma should want to be born as an outcaste! That he should love scavenging! He loved the man. He felt he could put his life in his hands and ask him to do what he liked with it. For him he would do anything. He would like to go and be a scavenger at his *ashram*. 'Then I could talk to him,' he said to himself. 'But I am not listening, I am not listening; I must listen.'

'If there are any Untouchables here,' he heard the Mahatma say, 'they should realise that they are cleaning Hindu society.' (He felt like shouting to say that he, an Untouchable, was there, but he did not know what the Mahatma meant by 'cleaning Hindu society.') He gave ear to the words with beating heart and heard: 'They have, therefore, to purify their lives. They should cultivate the habits of cleanliness, so that no one shall point his finger at them. Some of them are addicted to habits of drinking and gambling of which they must get rid.

'They claim to be Hindus. They read the scriptures. If,

therefore, the Hindus oppress them, they should understand that the fault does not lie in the Hindu religion, but in those who profess it. In order to emancipate themselves they have to purify themselves. They have to rid themselves of evil habits, like drinking liquor and eating carrion.'

But now, now the Mahatma is blaming us, Bakha felt. 'That is not fair!' He wanted to forget the last passages that he had heard. He turned to the Mahatma.

'They should now cease to accept leavings from the plates of high-caste Hindus, however clean they may be represented to be. They should receive grain only—good, sound grain, not rotten grain—and that too, only if it is courteously offered. If they are able to do all that I have asked them to do, they will secure their emancipation.'

That was more to Bakha's liking. He felt that he wanted to turn round and say to the Mahatma: 'Now, Mahatma ji, now you are talking.' He felt he would like to tell him that that very day, in that very town where he was speaking, he (Bakha) had had to pick up a loaf of bread from near the gutter; that to-day, there, in that very city, his brother had had to accept leavings of food from the plates of the sepoys, and that they had all to eat it. Bakha saw himself pitied by the Mahatma in his mind's eye and consoled by him. It was such a balm, it was so comforting, the great man's sympathy. 'If only he could go and tell my father not to be hard on me! If only he could go and tell him how I have suffered, if only he could go and tell my father he sympathises with me in my sufferings, my father would at once take me back and be kind to me ever afterwards.'

'I am an orthodox Hindu and I know that the Hindus are not sinful by nature,' Bakha heard the Mahatma declaim. 'They are sunk in ignorance. All public wells, temples, roads, schools, sanatoriums, must be declared open to the Untouchables. And, if you all profess to love me, give me a direct proof of your love by carrying on propaganda against the observance of untouchability. Do this, but let there be no compulsion or brute force in securing this end. Peaceful persuasion is the only means. Two of the strongest desires that keep me in the flesh are the emancipation of the Untouchables and the protection of the cow. When these two desires are fulfilled there is *swaraj*, and therein lies my soul's deliverance. May God give you strength to work out your soul's salvation to the end.'

When the crowd scattered irreverently at the end of the Mahatma's speech, Bakha stood on the branch of the tree spellbound. Each word, of the concluding passage seemed to him to echo as deep and intense a feeling of horror and indignation as his own at the distinction which the caste Hindus made between themselves and the Untouchables. The Mahatma seemed to have touched the most intimate corner of his soul. 'Surely he is a good man,' Bakha said.

Muffled cries of 'Mahatma ji ki-jai,' 'Hindu—Mussulman ki-jai,' 'Harijan ki-jai' arose from the middle of the throng again, and Bakha knew that the sage was going from the platform to the gate. He clung to his position on the tree, and was rewarded for his patience by the sight of the Mahatma passing beneath him.

A man seated on a high wooden board, with a bucket beside him, was distributing water in a silver tankard to Muhammadans in red fezes and Hindus in white Gandhi caps.

'He has made Hindu and Mussulman one,' remarked a citizen, surcharged with the glow of brotherliness and humanitarianism which the Mahatma had left in his trail.

'Let's discard foreign cloth. Let's burn it!' the Congress volunteers were shouting. And true enough, Bakha saw people throwing their felt caps, their silk shirts and aprons into the pile, which soon became a blazing bonfire.

'Sister,' said another citizen to a grass-cutter's wife, who struggled in her heavy accordion-pleated skirt to take her two children home, 'let me help you through the crowd. Give me the big boy to hold.'

There was only one queer voice which dissented from all this.

'Gandhi is a humbug,' it was saying. 'He is a fool. He is a hypocrite. In one breath he says he wants to abolish untouchability, in the other he asserts that he is an orthodox Hindu. He is running counter to the spirit of our age, which is democracy. He is in the fourth century B.C. with his *swadeshi* and his spinning-wheel. We live in the twentieth. I have read Rousseau, Hobbes, Bentham and John Stuart Mill and I . . .'

Bakha came down the tree like a black bear, and arrested the democrat's attention by the ridiculous sight he presented. He was going to slink away shyly, but the man, a fair-complexioned Muhammadan dressed in the most smartly-cut English suit he had ever seen, interrupted him:

'Eh, eh, black man, come here. Go and get a bottle of soda-water for the sahib.'

Bakha came back with a start and stood staring at the dignitary who had called him. The man wore a monocle in his left eye and Bakha, who had never seen anything of that kind, wondered how a single glass could remain fixed on the eye without a frame.

'Don't stare at me!' shouted the gentleman, while Bakha was wondering who the man could be, too sallow-faced for an Englishman, too white for an Indian, and clad in such fine clothes, yellow gloves on his hands and white cloth on his buckskin shoes.

'*Ham desi sahib* (I, native sahib), don't stare at me,' said the man deliberately using the wrong Hindustani spoken by the English, but becoming kinder for a moment. 'I have just come from *Vilayat* (England). Is there a sodawater shop near here?'

Bakha had been taken unawares. He couldn't adjust himself to this phenomenon. So he moved his head to indicate that he didn't know. Fortunately for him the man's attention was switched off to his friend, a young man with a delicate feline face, illuminated by sparkling dark eyes and long black curly hair, who stood next to him dressed in flowing Indian robes like a poet's. Bakha's inadequate answer did not, therefore, evoke the insolent flourish of the democrat's cane as it might have done.

'It is very unfair of you to abuse the Mahatma,' Bakha heard the young poet say gently, as he walked a little way away from the two men who were now surrounded by a group of people. 'He is by far the, greatest liberating force of our age. He has his limits, of course. But . . .'

'Precisely,' Bakha heard his companion interrupt. 'That is exactly what I say. And my contention is . . .'

'Yes, but listen, I haven't finished,' the poet was saying. 'He has his limitations but he is fundamentally sound. He may be wrong in wanting to shut India off from the rest of the world by preaching the revival of the spinning-wheel, because, as things are, that can't be done. But even in that regard he is right. For it is not India's fault that it is poor; it is the world's fault that the world is rich! . . .'

'You are talking in paradoxes. You have been reading Shaw,' interrupted, the monocled gentleman.

'Oh, forget Shaw! I am not a decadent Indian like you to be pandering to those European film stars!' exclaimed the poet. 'But you know that it is only in terms of economic theory that India is behind the other countries of the world. In fact, it is one of the richest countries; it has abundant natural resources. Only it has chosen to remain agricultural and has suffered for not accepting the machine. We must, of course, remedy that. I hate the machine. I loathe it. But I shall go against Gandhi there and accept it. And I am sure in time all will learn to love it. And we shall beat our enslavers at their own game . . .'

'They will put you into prison,' someone interrupted from the crowd.

'Never mind that. I am not afraid of prison. I have already been a guest at His Majesty's boarding-house with a hundred thousand others who were imprisoned last year . . .'

'The peasant who believes this world to be *maya* (illusion) will not work the machine,' remarked the supercilious man in spats, as he adjusted his monocle to reflect the cynical glint in his eye.

'It is India's genius to accept all things,' said the poet fiercely. 'We have, throughout our long history, been realists believing in the stuff of this world, in the here and the now, in the flesh and the blood. Man is born, and reborn, according to the *Upanishads*, in this world, and even when he becomes an immortal saint there is no release for him, because he forms the stuff of the cosmos and is born again. We don't believe in the other world, as these Europeans would have you believe we do. There has been only one man in India who believed this world to be illusory—Shankaracharya. But he was a consumptive and that made him neurotic. Early European scholars could not get hold of the original texts of the *Upanishads*. So they kept on interpreting Indian thought from the commentaries of Shankaracharya. The word *maya* does not mean illusion, it means magic. That is the dictum of the latest Hindu translator of the *Vedanta*, Dr. Coomaraswamy. And in that signification the word approximates to the views on the nature of the physical world of your pet scientists, Eddington and Jeans. The Victorians misinterpreted us. It was as if, in order to give a philosophical background to their exploitation of India, they ingeniously concocted a nice little fairy story: "You don't believe in this world; to you all this is *maya*. Let us look after your country for you and you can dedicate yourself to achieving *Nirvana* (release from the trammels of existence)." But that is all over now. Right in the tradition of those who accepted the world and produced the baroque exuberance of Indian architecture and sculpture, with its profound sense of form, its solidity and its mass, we will accept and work the machine. But we will do so consciously. We can see through the idiocy of these Europeans who deified money. They were barbarians and lost their heads in the worship of gold. We can steer clear of the pitfalls, because we have the advantage of a race-consciousness six thousand years old, a race-consciousness which accepted all the visible and invisible values. We know life. We know its secret flow. We have danced to its rhythms. We have loved it, not sentimentally through personal feelings, but

143

pervasively, stretching ourselves from our hearts outwards so far, oh, so far, that life seemed to have no limits, that miracles seemed possible. We can feel new feelings. We can learn to be aware with a new awareness. We can envisage the possibility of creating new races from the latent heat in our dark brown bodies. Life is still an adventure for us. We are still eager to learn. We cannot go wrong. Our enslavers muddle through things. We can see things clearly. We will go the whole hog with regard to machines while they nervously fumble their way with the steam-engine. And we will keep our heads through it all. We will not become slaves to gold. We can be trusted to see life steadily and see it whole.'

The harangue was impressive, with such fire was it delivered. Not only was the crowd moved but the anglicised Indian was silenced. Bakha was too much under the spell of Gandhi to listen intently to anyone else, and he did not follow all that the poet said although he strained to catch his words.

'Who is he?' someone in the crowd queried.

'Iqbal Nath Sarshar, the young poet who edits the *Nawan Jug* (*New Era*). and his companion is Mr. R.N. Bashir, B.A. (Oxon.), Barrister-at-Law,' someone volunteered the information.

There were whispers of consent and appreciation, but Mr. Bashir's voice rose above the others in a derisive little chuckle.

'Ha, ha, ho ho! but what has all this got to do with untouchability? Gandhi's plea is an expression of his inferiority complex. I think . . .'

'I know what you think,' put in the poet fiercely, exciting some amusement with his brisk retort. 'Let me tell you that with regard to untouchability the Mahatma is more sound than he is in his political and economic views. You have swallowed all those cheap phrases about inferiority complex and superiority complex at Oxford without understanding what they mean. You slavishly copy the English in everything . . .'

'That's right!' shouted a Congress volunteer. 'Look at his silk neck-tie and the suit of foreign cloth that he is wearing! Shame!'

'The heredity and the environment of different people varies,' continued the poet with a flourish of his hand to still the rude Congress wallah. 'Some of us are born with big heads, some with small, some with more potential physical strength, some with less. There is one saint to a hundred million people perhaps, one great man to a whole lot of mediocrities. But essentially, that is to say humanly, all men are equal. "Take a ploughman from the plough, wash off his dirt, and he is fit to rule a kingdom" is an old Indian proverb. The civility, the understanding and the gravity of the poorest of our peasants is a proof of that. Go and talk to a yokel and see how kind he is, how full of compliment, and how elegantly he speaks. And the equality of man is no new notion for him. If it had not been for ride the wily Brahmins, the priestcraft, who came in the pride of their white skin, lifted the pure philosophical idea of *Karma*, that deeds and acts are dynamic, that all is in a flux, from the Dravidians, and misinterpreted it vulgarly to mean that birth and rebirth in this universe is governed by good or bad deeds in the past life, India would have offered the best instance of a democracy. As it is, caste is an intellectual aristocracy, based on the conceit of the pundits, being otherwise wholly democratic. The high-caste High Court Judge eats freely with the coolie of his caste. So we can destroy our inequalities easily. The old mechanical formulas of our lives must go, the old stereotyped forms must give place to a new dynamism. We Indians live so deeply in our contacts; we are so acutely aware of our blood-stream . . .'

'I can't understand what you mean,' interrupted Bashir irritatedly.

'Well, we must destroy caste, we must destroy the inequalities of birth and unalterable vocations. We must recognise an equality of rights, privileges and opportunities for everyone. The Mahatma didn't say so, but the legal and sociological basis of caste having been broken down by the British-Indian penal code, which recognises the rights of every man before a court, caste is now mainly governed by profession. When the sweepers change their profession, they will no longer remain Untouchables. And they can do that soon, for the first thing we will do when we accept the machine, will be to introduce the machine which clears dung without anyone having to handle it—the flush system. Then the sweepers can be free from the stigma of untouchability and assume the dignity of status that is their right as useful members of a casteless and classless society.'

'In fact,' mocked Bashir, 'greater efficiency, better salesmanship, more mass-production, standardisation, dictatorship of the sweepers, Marxian materialism and all that!'

'Yes, yes, all that, but no catch-words and cheap phrases. The change will be organic and not mechanical.'

'All right, all right, come, don't let us stand here, I feel suffocated,' said Mr. Bashir, pulling out a silken handkerchief to wipe his face.

The crowd looked, ogled, stared with wonder at the celebrities and followed them at a little distance, till they disappeared in the unending throng of people going out of the golbagh.

Bakha had stood aside, beyond polluting distance, thinking vaguely of the few things he had understood from the poet's outburst. He felt that the poet would have been answering the most intimate questions in his (Bakha's) soul, if he had not used such big words. 'That machine,' he thought, 'which can remove dung without anyone having to handle it, I wonder what it is like? If only that "gentreman" hadn't dragged the poet away, I could have asked him.'

The fires of sunset were blazing on the western horizon. As Bakha looked at the magnificent orb of terrible brightness glowing on the margin of the sky, he felt a burning sensation within him. His face, which had paled and contracted with thoughts a moment ago, reddened in a curious conflict of despair. He didn't know what to do, where to go. He seemed to have been smothered by the misery, the anguish of the morning's memories. He stood for a while where he had landed from the tree, his head bent, as if he were tired and broken. Then the last words of the Mahatma's speech seemed to resound in his ears: 'May God give you the strength to work out your soul's salvation to the end.' 'What did that mean?' Bakha asked himself. The Mahatma's face appeared before him enigmatic, ubiquitous. There was no answer to be found in it. Yet there was a queer kind of strength to be derived from it. Bakha recollected the words of his speech. It all seemed to stand out in his mind, every bit of it. Specially'did the story of Uka come back. The Mahatma had talked of a Brahmin who did the scavenging in his *ashram*. 'Did he mean, then, that I should go on scavenging?' Bakha asked himself.

'Yes,' came the forceful answer. 'Yes,' said Bakha, 'I shall go on doing what Gandhi says.' 'But shall I never be able to leave the latrines? 'came the disturbing thought. But I can. Did not that poet say there is a machine which can do my work?' The prospect of never being able to wear the clothes that the sahibs wore, of never being able to become a sahib, was horrible. 'But it doesn't matter,' he said to console himself, and pictured in his mind the English policeman, whom he had seen before the meeting, standing there, ignored by everybody.

He began to move. His virtues lay in his close-knit sinews and in his long-breathed sense. He was thinking of everything he had heard though he could not understand it all. He was calm as he walked along, though the conflict in his soul was not over, though he was torn between his enthusiasm for Gandhi and the difficulties in his own awkward, naïve self.

The sun descended. The pale, the purple, the mauve of the horizon blended into darkest blue. A handful of stars throbbed in the heart of the sky.

He emerged from the green of the garden into the slight haze of dust that rose from the roads and the paths.

As the brief Indian twilight came and went, a sudden impulse shot through the transformations of space and time, and gathered all the elements that were dispersed in the stream of his soul into a tentative decision: 'I shall go and tell father all that Gandhi said about us,' he whispered to himself, 'and all that that poet said. Perhaps I can find the poet some day and ask him about his machine.' And he proceeded homewards.